# Bella
## Broomstick

# STRICTLY
# SPELLS

# Bella Broomstick

## STRICTLY SPELLS

### LOU KUENZLER

ILLUSTRATED BY

KYAN CHENG

**SCHOLASTIC**

Scholastic Children's Books
An imprint of Scholastic Ltd
Euston House, 24 Eversholt Street, London, NW1 1DB, UK
Registered office: Westfield Road, Southam, Warwickshire, CV47 0RA
SCHOLASTIC and associated logos are trademarks and/or
registered trademarks of Scholastic Inc.

First published in the UK by Scholastic Ltd, 2017

Text copyright © Lou Kuenzler, 2017

The right of Lou Kuenzler to be identified as the author
of this work has been asserted by her.

ISBN 978 1407 18100 4

A CIP catalogue record for this book
is available from the British Library.

Printed by CPI Group (UK) Ltd, Croydon, CR0 4YY
Papers used by Scholastic Children's Books are made
from wood grown in sustainable forests.

1 3 5 7 9 10 8 6 4 2

This is a work of fiction. Names, characters, places, incidents
and dialogues are products of the author's imagination or are used
fictitiously. Any resemblance to actual people, living or dead,
~~events or locales is entirely coincidental.~~

# Chapter One

I woke up slowly, rolled over in bed and opened my eyes as pale winter sunlight streamed through my bedroom curtains. It was New Year's Day – my first one in Merrymeet Village. I lay still for a moment, thinking how lucky I was to live here with my wonderful foster parents, Aunty Rose and Uncle Martin. A whole fresh year lay ahead of us – 365 brilliant new days together. And I didn't want to waste another

1

single second in bed! I sat up, yawned and stretched my arms.

"Blundering bullfrogs!" I gasped as my best friend, Esme, charged across the room and leapt on the end of the bed.

I had completely forgotten she had stayed for a sleepover.

"Happy New Year!" Esme whooped. And, before I could answer, she tweaked my nose and thumped me HARD on the arm.

"Ouch!" I cried in surprise. "What did you do that for?"

"Pinch, punch, first of the month!" Esme waved my Aunty Rose's brand-new *Strictly Sequins* ballroom dancing calendar at me. "It's the first of January, silly!"

She bounced up and down on the bed, pointing to the date – which was right below an enormous, shiny picture of Ken Smyles, the host of the *Strictly Sequins* dance show on telly-vision. He had bright white smile on his face and wore a sparkly silver suit covered in a thousand twinkly sequins.

Aunty Rose loves Ken Smyles. I gave her the calendar for Christmas and she said she was "tickled-pink"! I wasn't sure what that meant, but I know she was pleased as her cheeks went all rosy with excitement. She *really* does love Ken!

"You better put that calendar back in the kitchen before it gets ripped," I said to Esme, rubbing my arm grumpily. "I don't see what *Strictly Sequins* has got to do with you punching me."

"Oh, I'm sorry. I didn't mean to hurt you, Bella." Esme gave my arm a comforting pat. "Don't you do *pinch punch* in the Magic Realm?" My face must have looked blank because Esme smiled sympathetically and explained, "It's just a silly tradition we do here on the first of every month."

"Ah," I said. "I understand." But I didn't. Not really. In fact, most Person World traditions are a mystery to me.

You see, the problem is, I'm a witch.

What I used to look like
when I lived in the
Magic Realm

What I look like now,
in the Person World

I've only been living in Merrymeet since
the end of the summer, and before that I
lived in the Magic Realm with my mean
Aunt Hemlock. Getting used to peculiar
Person ways is a bit of a shock. I'm getting
better at it, but I'm not sure I'll ever get
used to all the strange customs here – like

telling knock–knock jokes, saying "BOO!" to cure hiccups or touching wood for good luck.

Esme was still looking guilty and rubbing my arm. "Don't worry!" I grinned. "It's not that bad. It's not as if you turned me into a toad or anything."

"Which is what you did to *me*, last term!" Esme giggled, reminding me of the time I'd turned her into a toad – and then almost lost her in a muddy stream. She is just about the only Person in the whole village who knows that I am secretly a witch.

"Here," I said, reaching over to my bedside table and giving her the last chocolate coin, which I had been saving from my Christmas stocking. "Have this." I know Esme loves chocolate – and it would prove there were no hard feelings for the pinch punch.

"Ooh, thank you!" She took the chocolate and was about to unwrap it. Then she gasped suddenly. "I forgot — I can't! I was thinking about giving up sweets as my New Year's resolution."

I stared at her.

"Oh — you won't have heard of that either. Well, because it's the first of January, we should make a resolution and decide to do something good to start the new year," she explained. "I was thinking about giving up sweets."

"Giving up sweets?" Galloping Goblins! Why would Esme want to do something like that? Sweets are one of my favourite things about the Person World. When I was growing up in the Magic Realm, my horrible witchy Aunt Hemlock's idea of a treat was to dip a slug in vinegar and suck it or crunch a box of salted snails. She did give me a lollipop once – when I was five – but when I licked it, it turned out to be a curled-up worm.

"Sweets in the Person World are SO delicious," I said.

"That's the point of a New Year's resolution," Esme explained. "It has to be something that's hard to do… Last year I gave up biting my nails." She held out her hands, then quickly bunched them up again. "That didn't go too well."

"But … I could never give up sweets.

Not for a whole year." There were still so many different Person treats I hadn't tried. Piers Seymour, the boy who lives next door, told me about something wonderful called a gobstopper which is supposed to be as big as a tennis ball. But you can never be sure with Piers – he might have been making it up.

"A resolution doesn't have to last for a whole year," said Esme. "A month will do."

"A *month*?" That seemed bad enough.

But Esme leapt to her feet. "Yes! That's it – I've decided. My New Year's resolution is to give up sweets for the whole of January," she said. "But not just sweets. Chocolate too. And fudge, and toffee, and marshmallows and lollipops and. . ."

"Stop!" She was making my mouth water just thinking about it. "You won't want my chocolate coin, then." I smiled. "Can

I have it back?"

"No chance!" Esme slipped it into her dressing gown pocket with a cheeky grin. "I'll save it till the first of February. It's mine now. You gave it to me!"

"Hmm, we'll see about that," I teased her, rummaging under my pillow. I pulled out my fluffy pink-flamingo feather pen. Underneath all that fluff it might look like an ordinary biro, but it is really a magic wand. "I can get my chocolate back whenever I want. I'm a witch, remember?"

I waved the wand towards Esme's dressing gown pocket and muttered a little spell:

*Bring me back my chocolate treat*
*I really fancy something sweet. . .*

Whoosh! Bright light in every colour of the rainbow shot out the end of my pen.

POW! Red, yellow and orange sparks rocked the door.

PING! Blue, indigo and violet waves rattled the window.

PONG! Thick green fog swirled in circles all around us like billowing smoke.

"Crazy crocodiles!" I coughed. "I wasn't expecting that." Something was wrong. My fun magic had exploded like an angry volcano.

"What's going on?" cried my little kitten, Rascal, who had been asleep on my chair. His hair stood on end like a startled porcupine as he darted under the wardrobe to hide.

"Sorry... Just a little magic!" I explained, calling to him in Cat Chat, which I speak fluently. I staggered to the window, flung it open and let the furious, spinning spell escape into the misty morning air.

"Look!" Esme coughed. "The magic didn't even work. I've still got the chocolate coin you gave me. See?" I caught a glimpse of gold foil as she waved it in the air.

"Walloping Warlocks! I've been so silly," I groaned, steadying myself against the window frame. "I should have remembered. A witch cannot use magic to get something back once she has freely given it away. No spell, no matter how powerful, could ever have got that chocolate back... Unless you don't want it any more?" I said hopefully. "That's the only way I could ever take it back."

"Well, bad luck!" said Esme firmly. "You've given it to me now and I most certainly do want it. I'm going to eat it on the first of February at one minute past midnight!" She smiled and popped the coin into her pocket again as the last sparks of the spell shot out of the window.

"Thumping Thunderbolts! That was a close one!" I said, fanning the air with the *Strictly Sequins* calendar. "I thought the whole room was going to explode." But, the moment I spoke, the door opened and Aunty Rose popped her head inside.

"Are you all right in here, girls? I heard a terrible noise," she said.

"Erm, we're fine!" I squealed. Although, I spotted a long-burnt scorch mark all along the windowsill which I tried to hide with a pile of books. Thank goodness the last of the swirling magic had vanished or it might have given away my secret. Aunty Rose and Uncle Martin have no idea that I am a witch and I don't want them to find out. "We were just – er..."

"Practising a dance routine," said Esme, tossing the sparkly calendar to Aunty Rose as she grabbed me by the waist and waltzed me around the room.

"Whoops!" Aunty Rose leapt out of the way. "As long as you're having fun... Just don't dance right through the floor," she warned us as she backed out of the door and closed it behind her.

"We won't!" I called, sinking into a heap on my bedroom carpet. "Well done, Esme! That was super-quick thinking," I whispered. I am always terrified Aunty Rose and Uncle Martin won't want to foster me any more if they find out they've given a home to a witch.

"I should know better than to play with spells in my bedroom," I groaned. Doing magic in the Person World was just too much of a risk. I shouldn't use my wand at all in case

14

somebody sees me. But somehow I always get carried away. Especially when I'm with Esme. She makes doing magic so much fun.

"It's all very well for you!" hissed Rascal, crawling out from under the wardrobe. "But look at my tail!"

"Oh no! You poor thing," I purred. The tip of his soft grey fur was singed black as a witch's hat. I scooped him up in my arms and kissed the end of his nose.

"That's it!" I said firmly, as Esme flopped on to the floor beside me. "I know what I'm going to do for my New Year's resolution. And it's not giving up sweets!"

"What is it, then?" she asked.

"I'm going to give up magic, of course," I said.

"Good thing too!" huffed Rascal. And he was right. I would begin the new year as I meant to go on.

"No more spells for a whole month!" I promised. "Starting right now!"

# Chapter Two

Esme and I didn't get a chance to talk any more about our New Year's resolutions before Aunty Rose called us downstairs. She'd made pancakes for breakfast.

I had chocolate spread and sprinkles on mine. Because Esme had given up sweets, she decided she better have plain banana on hers – but she said it was delicious anyway.

It was a lovely, frosty morning and, as soon as we were finished, I asked Esme if she wanted to go for a walk to the top of Merrymeet Hill.

"I've got a plan, but I can't tell you about it here." I whispered to her under my breath. I had thought of the perfect way to make sure that I didn't do any magic for a whole month. Not even by mistake.

"All right," said Esme. And, when we asked Aunty Rose and Uncle Martin, they agreed we could go.

"Just make sure you wrap up warm," said Uncle Martin. "Shall I make you a nice hot flask of tea to take?"

He picked up the kettle, but I could see he already had a packet of sunflower seeds under his arm, ready to go out and feed the birds in the garden. He always likes to give them something extra when it's cold.

"Don't worry," I said. "We'll be fine."

"How about some sandwiches?" asked Aunty Rose, looking up from a magazine.

"No, thanks. We've eaten loads of pancakes," I said, before she could jump up and start making something. "You enjoy your magazine." She was reading about all Ken Smyles from *Strictly Sequins*. He was grinning out of the page with his famous big white teeth and bright orange tan. I always think he looks a bit like a smiley pumpkin ... but Aunty Rose adores him.

"Tada, da, da, da," she sang, swaying in her chair. Aunty Rose hardly ever puts her feet up. She is always too busy worrying about me – just like Uncle Martin. No matter what they're doing, they always find time to help – offering me lifts, taking me shopping, checking I've had enough to eat – loving and caring for me in every way, just as if I were their real daughter.

I kissed her cheek. "Thank you! And Happy New Year to you both!" I called with a rush of happiness, as I buttoned up the beautiful big red coat they had given me for Christmas. "See you later."

Esme and I hurried out the door.

"Go on then," she puffed as we climbed the footpath to the top of Merrymeet Hill. "Tell me about this secret plan of yours..."

Ten minutes later, we stood on the very top of the hill with the wind blowing all around us.

Esme was staring at me as if I was mad.

"Say that again," she said. "You're going to do *what*?"

"I am going to turn my wand back into a real flamingo," I said, pulling the fluffy pen out of my pocket. "And then——"

"And then you're going to let it go," Esme interrupted. "So it can fly off somewhere warm for a month's holiday."

"Exactly!" Uncle Martin had told me flamingos often come from hot, sunny places, so I knew she'd be happy to have a nice warm break. "The most important thing is that I send my wand far away, so that I can't use it until the first of February. Then I'll call her back again," I explained.

"I don't understand," Esme said. "You've promised not to use your wand for a whole month anyway."

"I know. But I need to be sure," I

said. "I've been getting so careless lately. Look at what happened this morning. I didn't even think twice before I cast that chocolate coin spell. Aunty Rose almost caught me. Poor Rascal was nearly singed to a crisp. And I was lucky the whole cottage didn't explode!"

"It was only a bit of fun," said Esme.

"Magical fun!" I sighed. "And that always causes trouble in the Person World. Just remember Halloween."

"Don't remind me!" Esme began to chew her nails.

Halloween had been HORRIBLE ... but it had all started out as a bit of fun. I had cast a spell so me and Esme and poor little Rascal could fly on a broomstick. Unfortunately, I accidentally took us all to the Magic Realm where my evil Aunt Hemlock kidnapped Esme and tried to turn

us all to stone. It was an AWFUL night –
and we were lucky to escape at all.

"I want to start the New Year without
any sort of magic trouble," I said. "With
this one last spell I can send my wand away
for a lovely little holiday in the sun. One
whole month, then she'll be back."

"But you'll miss magic so much," said
Esme. "You love it."

"And you love sweets," I said. "But you're
giving them up for a whole month too." I
stroked the soft pink pen feathers against my
cheek. Esme was right. I really did love doing
magic. I had got quite good at it with my new
flamingo wand – except for a few unexpected
fireworks like this morning… I thought of
poor Rascal's singed tail and that terrifying
Halloween trip to the Magic Realm. Spells
in the Person World had a terrible way of
causing trouble – a nice long break would

do me good. I knew what I had to do.

Before I could change my mind, I kissed the top of the flamingo's plastic head, then held the pen up to the sky:

> Turn back to a bird and fly away
> Somewhere warm for a holiday.
> Go freely till the month is done,
> Spread your wings and have
> some fun.

Whoosh! The wand shot out of my hand. There was a flutter of feathers, and a real flamingo circled above us in the sky. I raised my arm and waved. Then, with a streak of sparkly pink lightning, she was gone. Up, up, up into the clouds.

We stared at the grey

sky as the beautiful bird flew off towards the pale sun. The wind rustled her feathers as she went.

"See you in a month," I whispered, and I blew a kiss.

"Goodbye!" cried Esme.

"Come on," I said, when the last flicker of pink had vanished into the clouds. "Let's go home." My heart was pounding as I realized the full power of what I had done. Having my wand had always made me feel safe. Without it, I couldn't do magic even if I wanted to. Even if I *needed* to... But there was nothing to worry about. Not here in the Person World. And it was only for a month. Surely nothing too terrible would happen in that short time...

# Chapter Three

The thing I love about having a best friend is that Esme always seems to know how I am feeling.

She guessed at once how sad I must be about letting my wand go.

"Come on!" she said, slipping her arm through mine. "You're right. It's only for a month. And think of all the delicious sweets you can eat while I can't have any. . . Cherry drops!" She sighed dramatically.

"Gummy beans, white chocolate, gobstoppers. . ."

"Gobstoppers? So they're real?" I asked.

"Of course gobstoppers are real!" Esme laughed. "They sell them in Merrymeet Sweet Shop. They're as big as tennis balls."

"Blistering Boulders! That's what Piers said. I can't wait to try one!" I cried. Piers Seymour used to be our worst enemy. He was always spying on me from his big house next door and bullying Esme because her family don't have much money. Then I helped him out with a little magic on his Halloween costume and we became friends.

"Piers was telling the truth." Esme smiled. "You know he's a changed boy ever since he found out you really are a witch."

"Shh!" I said, looking around. "Someone

27

might hear you."

"There's no one else here," said Esme, laughing and looking around the deserted hillside. But the moment she spoke, the trees around us shivered and the wind began to howl. My cheeks stung as if invisible icy fingers had touched my face. And a low grey mist slunk around our ankles like a serpent.

"What is it?" cried Esme. "What's happening?"

"I don't know. But it feels like magic. Bad magic," I said, reaching into my pocket to grab my wand before remembering I didn't have it. I swallowed. There was nothing I could do. No way I could protect us from whatever this cold, strange sorcery was.

There was a rushing sound, like the swoosh of wings. I looked up into the sky, hoping that it was my flamingo, sensing danger and coming back to help us.

But it wasn't a flash of pink I saw.

There was a blast of bright white lightning – then a black shadow. Something was coming this way – something I recognized.

Whoosh!

Before I could warn Esme about what it was, a cloaked figure riding a broomstick landed right beside us on the hill.

"Well, well, Belladonna!" A witch in a dark pointy hat stared deep into my eyes. She was so close, I could feel her icy breath on my skin.

"Aunt Hemlock!" I gasped. "What are you doing here in the Person World?"

"Why, I've come to see you, of course!" she said with a nasty laugh. "Can't an aunt pay a little visit to her niece?"

"But..." I didn't trust Aunt Hemlock for a moment. She had never come to visit me

before. In fact she had been only too glad to get rid of me when she banished me from the Magic Realm all those months ago.

Her broomstick was hovering behind her in mid-air. She folded her arms and perched on it as if she was resting on a park bench.

It was hopeless to try and run. Whatever it was she wanted, Aunt Hemlock could simply cast a spell and make me freeze on the spot. My stomach twisted like a sack of snakes. Without my wand, I couldn't protect myself and I couldn't protect Esme either – all because of my silly New Year's resolution.

"All right… You can talk to me if you have to," I stammered, swallowing hard and hoping she couldn't see my knees shaking under my coat. "But my friend needs to go… Don't you?" I turned towards Esme, who was as white as a marshmallow and chewing her fingernails again. It was hardly surprising. The last time she had seen Aunt Hemlock, Esme had been held prisoner and nearly turned to stone. "You've got a . . . a. . ." My brain was frozen. I tried to think of a good excuse to send Esme away. Then Aunty Rose's calendar flashed into my mind – the one with all the contestants from *Strictly Sequins* swirling across the page. "You've got a . . . a ballroom dancing lesson," I blurted out at last.

"Ballroom dancing?" Esme spluttered. "I don't do ballroom dancing. . ."

"Yes, you do!" I said. "And you need to go to your lesson. RIGHT NOW!"

There was still no sign of anyone else up here – even the birds seemed to have stopped singing as the cold grey mist smothered the hilltop like a cloak.

"I'm not going anywhere," said Esme

firmly. "I'm staying here with you!" Her voice was shaking but she took my hand. "My ballroom dancing has been ... er ... cancelled."

"Stay. Go. *Turn into* a dancing leprechaun for all I care," said Aunt Hemlock. But she was peering at Esme very strangely now. "Don't I know you, Person-child? Haven't I seen you somewhere before?"

"That's impossible," I said quickly. After we escaped from the Magic Realm at Halloween I cast a forgetfulness spell so the witches would never know Esme had secretly visited their world or that I had used magic against them.

"Hmm." Aunt Hemlock scratched her warty nose. "The Person-child is of no interest to me anyway. Come along, Belladonna!" Aunt Hemlock tapped the back of the broomstick with her long, thin nails. "It's time to go."

"*Go?*" I gasped. "Where to?"

"Back to the Magic Realm, of course," Aunt Hemlock cackled. "Didn't I tell you, Belladonna Broomstick? You are coming home with me."

# Chapter Four

Time seemed to stand still.

I opened and closed my mouth like a goldfish, trying to take in Aunt Hemlock's words.

"You want me to come back to the Magic Realm?" I said. Ice-cold fear pricked my skin. "You're going to make me leave the Person World? But I love it here. I've got friends."

Esme squeezed my hand.

"I won't let that old witch take you, Bella," she whispered. But I knew it was hopeless. Aunt Hemlock leant forward like a rattlesnake about to pounce.

"What about my foster parents – Aunty Rose and Uncle Martin?" I said, and my eyes filled up with tears. "I love them. And they love me."

"Love!" Aunt Hemlock threw back her head and laughed as if I had told a funny joke. "What's love got to with anything?"

"Everything!" said Esme.

"Silence!" roared Aunt Hemlock, reaching for her wand.

"Stop!" I stepped forward, shielding Esme behind me. It was stupid of me to try and tell Aunt Hemlock how I felt. I was wasting my time. Witches don't care about things like friendship or loyalty or love.

"I just can't understand why you want

me to come back to the Magic Realm," I said. Aunt Hemlock had never tired of telling me what a burden it was for her to have to bring me up ever since my parents accidentally turned themselves into white mice and disappeared when I was a baby.

"It's true that you've always been an embarrassment to me." Aunt Hemlock wrinkled her nose. "My silly little niece, the most hopeless witch in all of the Magic Realm."

"Exactly!" I said. That's why she banished me to the Person World in the first place. I was so bad at potions and spells back then, I failed the entrance to the Creepy Castle School of Witches and Wizards. She had no idea that I had found my flamingo wand when I first arrived in Merrymeet and learnt to do magic I would never have dreamed of. Not that it mattered now anyway – because my wonderful wand was long gone.

"Please," I beseeched her. "You don't want me back. You don't even like me."

"True. I don't like you." Aunt Hemlock narrowed her eyes. "But I do *miss* you..."

"You *miss* me?" I couldn't believe what I was hearing. Aunt Hemlock had never said anything even half nice to me in my whole life before.

"I *miss* having someone to sweep the cave," she hissed. "I *miss* having someone to scrub my cauldron." I should have known it. She wasn't being kind at all – she just wanted someone to do her chores. "I *miss* having someone to shout at when I'm bored," she cackled.

"Couldn't you pay someone to work for you?" said Esme desperately.

"Yes!" I agreed. It was a brilliant idea. "Perhaps a pixie or an elf?"

"They could do all those jobs in the cave and Bella could stay here," cried Esme.

"Pay?" Aunt Hemlock looked at her as if she was an idiot. "Why would I do that when Belladonna will work for free?"

"You want me to come back just so I can be your servant?" I said, with a heavy sense of dread filling my tummy. When Aunt Hemlock wants something, she always gets her own way.

"Yes! That's right! I knew you'd understand in the end." She laughed wildly.

If only I could get my wand back. Then maybe I could do something to stop her.

I pretended to cough and began to mutter a chant under my breath:

*Oh, magic wand, please return*
*And change this witch into a worm!*

I looked up and my heart leapt as there was a rustle of movement in the branches above me. Had it worked? Was the flamingo back? But I saw at once that it wasn't a bird up there at all. It was Aunt Hemlock's creepy chameleon, Wane. I should have known he'd be lurking somewhere nearby.

"Oh." I shivered. "It's only you."

"Charming!" He stuck his long tongue out at me and scuttled down the tree trunk.

I've always hated the way he can appear out of nowhere, changing colour and shifting shape in the gloom. When I lived in the Magic Realm, he was always disguising himself to spy on me and tell tales.

Aunt Hemlock stretched out her hand and he scurried up her sleeve to perch on her shoulder like a leathery parrot.

I should have realized it was hopeless to try and summon my wand. I had sent it away – freely – for the whole month. No spell could call it back.

Aunt Hemlock raised her own bone-white wand and pointed it straight at me.

So this was it. It was all over. My wonderful life in the Person World was finished ... the year ahead would not be filled with love and laughter, as I had hoped. I wouldn't be living with my lovely foster parents in their pretty cottage. I would be locked away in Aunt Hemlock's dark, damp cave. I wouldn't be watching telly-vision with Esme or baking cakes or sharing secrets ever again.

"Please," I begged. "Please, Aunt Hemlock, let me stay."

But she was already muttering a spell:

*Take this hopeless brat to my cave.*
*Send her there to be my slave...*

She waved her wand. One, two, three times...

Wane cheered. Esme screamed. There was a puff of purple smoke. I closed my eyes and then...

Nothing!

Nothing happened.

I opened my eyes again, very slowly, and saw that I wasn't in the Magic Realm. I was still standing on Merrymeet Hill, looking down towards the village.

"Wriggling Rats! It didn't work!" Aunt Hemlock was furious. She waved her wand again, almost howling like a wolf as she chanted the spell a second time.

*Take this hopeless brat to my cave.*
*Send her there to be my slave. . .*

Still nothing . . . except an even angrier puff of smoke. It was bright red now.

"I won't stand for this. You will come back to the Magic Realm with me," Aunt Hemlock wailed, raising her wand for the third time.

There was nothing but a tiny puff of green smoke that smelled like rotten eggs.

I froze. Wane screeched. Esme . . . giggled.

"Is something funny?" I gasped nervously. Had Esme gone mad? I couldn't understand why she was laughing. Not when Aunt

Hemlock was still pointing her wand straight at us.

But Esme just grinned from ear to ear. "She can't use magic to take you away with her, Bella. Don't you see?"

"No," I said. "I don't."

"What are you talking about, you pesky little Person?" Aunt Hemlock barked.

Esme jumped backwards at the power of her snarling voice, but she lifted her head and answered as slowly and calmly as if she were explaining the rules of a board game to her little sister. "It's obvious. You can't use magic to take Bella back with you," she said. "You gave her away when she came here, and what's been freely given can't be taken back." She grinned at me. "You're like the chocolate coin, silly!"

"Of course...!" It was just like my wand as well. "You're brilliant, Esme!" I squeezed her hand and turned to face Aunt Hemlock. My knees were shaking but I spoke up just as loud and clear as my brave friend.

"There is no spell strong enough to take me away from here," I said. "It's your own fault, Aunt Hemlock. You gave me up the day Aunty Rose and Uncle Martin agreed to foster me."

"Wretched brat!" Aunt Hemlock growled, sounding more like a wolf than ever. "You're right. It's unbreakable magic. I got shot of you ... and you were freely given away."

She took a step forward. Then a step back. Then another step forward again. For the first time in my life she seemed at a loss with what to do to me. She knew that there was no way round it. She had given me away and, as long as I was wanted here, no spell could take me back. She was beaten at last. And by her own magic too ... all those months ago when she had given me to my foster parents to keep.

"You wanted to be rid of me for ever. 'Good riddance!' That's what you said," I reminded her. "And now you've succeeded. No magic is powerful enough to take me away from Merrymeet. So long as Aunty Rose and Uncle Martin still want me, you can never take me back. Never!"

"Curse you!" spat Aunt Hemlock, but it sounded hollow. She grabbed her broomstick. Wane scuttled into the bristles and tried to hide. He knew his furious mistress would be in a boiling temper for days. Aunt Hemlock would probably set him to work scouring the cauldron and sponging the pans.

She snarled with rage, and I felt her icy breath on my skin once more. But I didn't move. I stared straight into her narrow green eyes. I wasn't frightened. Not any more.

"This isn't over, Belladonna," she hissed.

"Oh yes it is," I said. "You cannot take me back to the Magic Realm. You cannot bully me. You cannot frighten me ever again. Go home. And leave me alone."

My legs had stopped shaking. My fear had melted like frost on the ground. My fingers tingled with excitement. I was free from Aunt Hemlock. For ever.

"Fine! If that's what you want," she thundered. "Stay here and rot with your horrid foster Persons and your pathetic little pal." She climbed on to the broomstick. "I'll see that the Person-child doesn't remember any of this, of course. I don't want her squealing in the village about how she's seen a witch."

Before I could do anything, Aunt

Hemlock spun round and pointed her wand straight at Esme:

> *Make this Person forget what she*
> *has seen*
> *Witch and broomstick, all*
> *a dream...*

It was a forgetfulness spell. Just like the one I had used at Halloween.

Poof!

This time her magic worked.

Esme fell to the ground as Aunt Hemlock shot off like a furious, fizzling rocket into the sky.

"Good riddance, Belladonna Broomstick," she howled.

# Chapter Five

"Esme? Esme! Wake up."

I knelt beside my friend on the frosty grass with my heart pounding.

"Come on! Wake up ... pinch, punch, for the first of the month." I tweaked her nose and pummelled her arm.

"Ouch!" At last, Esme blinked and opened her eyes. "What did you do that for, Bella? It hurt!"

Before I could answer she sat up and

looked around. "Where am I? What are we doing up here on Merrymeet Hill? I thought I was going to stay at your house for a New Year sleepover?"

"You did. But you've forgotten," I said.

"Oh!" Esme scratched her head. "I had the strangest dream… There was a witch … a proper scary one, in a pointy hat. She had wobbly green warts on her nose." Esme shuddered.

"It wasn't a dream," I explained. "Aunt Hemlock was here. She came on her broomstick. But she's left now…" I glanced at the sky and felt a rush of relief. She really was gone. My heart slowed down a little at last. "She cast a spell to confuse you."

"Ah, a forgetfulness spell!" Esme nodded.

Most Persons wouldn't have believed a word I was saying, of course. Aunt Hemlock's spell would have worked, and they would think the whole thing was nothing more than a strange, scary dream. But Esme had been my friend for too long. And she had seen the Magic Realm for herself. She nodded as I told her everything that had happened.

"But that's brilliant," she said at last. "Don't you see? Aunt Hemlock will never come back for you again. She knows that magic cannot take you away from here. Not now you are part of a family who love you."

"You're right." I smiled as I helped Esme to her feet and spun her around as if we were dancing on *Strictly Sequins*. "I can live a normal life here in Merrymeet Village and never worry about the Magic Realm ever again. Instead, we can think about daft little things, like homework and you giving up sweets for a month." I was spinning her so fast that we both landed on our bottoms and fell over backwards on the soft grass.

"Whoops!" I giggled. "Perhaps it was a little soon for that." As I sat up I saw that Esme had buried her head in her hands.

"What's the matter?" I asked anxiously. "Are you still groggy from the spell?"

"It's not that." Esme lifted her head and sighed. "I just can't believe it... Did I really say I'd give up sweets? For a whole *month*?"

"I'm afraid so!" Poor Esme couldn't remember anything that had happened since the first moment we woke up. "Don't worry," I said. "It's only for thirty days."

"Thirty-one." Esme groaned. "January is a long month."

"All right, thirty-one," I agreed. "Then you'll be eating toffees galore and I'll have my beautiful flamingo wand back."

I grabbed Esme's hand and began to run

down the hill. "Come on!" All I could think about was getting back to Honeysuckle Cottage, the lovely little tumbledown home where I lived with Aunty Rose and Uncle Martin. I could stay there for ever now. Aunt Hemlock could never take me away from the Person World.

We pelted down the hill, racing each other. But as we reached the cottage, I skidded to a halt. There was a sudden flicker of black and white and a shrill screeching sound as a magpie landed on the top of the garden gate.

"Ark!"

"Fiery Phoenixes!" I gasped, nearly jumping out of my skin.

The scruffy bird ruffled its feathers and stared down at us both.

"Hello. You gave us quite a fright!" I

crowed, talking to it in Magpie (which is very similar to Raven or Rook). I can talk Owl as well. And Frog and Toad and Rat and Cat, of course. And Bat. Spider too. Any creature which you find in the Magic Realm. But either the magpie didn't understand, or it was ignoring me. It flew up to the apple tree and seemed to chuckle under its wing.

"Ark! Ark! Ark!"

Esme doesn't understand a word of Magpie – or any other animal language – but she was tugging my sleeve.

"Quick!" she said. "Salute and say 'Morning, Magpie', otherwise you'll get bad luck."

"Bad luck?" I must have looked confused because Esme smiled and took my arm.

"Don't worry. It's just another silly tradition," she explained. "A superstition. If you see a magpie on its own it's meant to be bad luck, *one for sorrow*."

"But if you salute it, the bad luck goes away?" I asked.

"It's meant to," said Esme.

I really didn't like the way the magpie was flapping from tree to tree, following us as we hurried up the garden path.

I stopped and touched the side of my head in a salute. "Morning, Magpie."

The next time I looked back, it was gone.

That evening, after Esme had gone back to her mum's, I sat on the sofa snuggled up between Aunty Rose and Uncle Martin watching the final of *Strictly Sequins* on telly-vision.

"Have a choccy," said Aunty Rose, opening the big tin she'd brought for Christmas. There were only a few left, but the sweets looked like jewels in their sparkly gold, sapphire-blue and ruby-red wrappers. There was even one of my favourite emerald-green triangles.

"Thank you," I said, popping it into my mouth and thinking about poor Esme, who wouldn't be able to eat any chocolate for a whole month. The green triangles were her favourite too.

"Look. It's the finale," said Aunty Rose, pointing to the telly-vision as all the contestants on the ballroom dancing show were swaying and swirling beneath a huge glittery globe. She was still holding the giant tin of sweets, but Uncle Martin leapt to his feet and waltzed her round the room, spilling toffees everywhere as they went.

"Ouch!" she cried as he trod on her toes. "Careful."

They did make a funny sight. Her head barely reached his shoulder − she was as plump and jolly as a cuddly armchair and he was tall and wavy, like a tree in a storm. They might not be brilliant at dancing, but it didn't matter. They were laughing and loving every moment. I was grinning from ear to ear too. They looked so happy and were having so much fun.

Then, as Aunty Rose collapsed back on the sofa, Uncle Martin grabbed my hand and we waltzed round the room too... At least, it was meant to be a waltz. I have seen a lot of strange Person dances, watching *Strictly Sequins* every week since

I first arrived here. But I don't think the steps Uncle Martin and I were doing would have scored many points from the judges.

"Ouch!" I yelped as he stood on my toe.

"Whoops! Sorry!" he cried, almost knocking over the lamp as he grabbed Aunty Rose again and we all spun around the room together.

"Oh dear!" Aunty Rose was laughing so hard, tears were streaming down her face. "One thing's for sure, none of us would ever win *Strictly Sequins*."

"Too true!" wheezed Uncle Martin. And we collapsed on to the sofa, spilling the chocolates all over the floor.

"Thank you," I said as we scrabbled around, putting the sweets back in the tin.

"For the dance?" Uncle Martin bowed like a fairy tale prince. "You're welcome!"

"No," I said. "For everything. For being

the very best foster parents in the whole world."

"Oh, sweetheart!" Aunty Rose blushed pink as the filling in a strawberry cream chocolate. "You know we love having you here."

"Of course we do," said Uncle Martin. "Honeysuckle Cottage is your home, Bella. It always will be. Nothing can ever change that."

"Thank yo—" I tried to speak. But I couldn't. There was a lump in my throat as big as a frog. Tears filled my eyes. They had no idea how everything could have changed for ever up there on the top of Merrymeet Hill. What if Aunt Hemlock really had managed to take me away? I would never have had fun family evenings like this ever again.

"There's no need to cry," teased Uncle

Martin. "Is our dancing really as bad as all that?"

"It's worse!" giggled Aunty Rose. "Much, much worse!" And we collapsed in fits of laughter all over again.

As *Strictly Sequins* finished on television, Uncle Martin went over to draw the curtains.

"Let's shut out this cold winter night," he said.

I jumped up to help. But as I looked out at the darkness, I froze.

The scruffy magpie was sitting on the windowsill, staring through the glass at us. It was as if it was watching us, watching the dancing show.

# Chapter Six

That night, I slept like a happy hibernating dragon. Even thoughts of the creepy magpie couldn't keep me awake.

When I woke up in the morning, I had a lovely warm feeling right down to the bottom of my toes.

Perhaps it was because Rascal (whose singed tail was quite recovered) was curled up on my feet.

Or perhaps it was because, for the first

time ever, Aunt Hemlock didn't have any power over me. Not even with magic.

"Oh, Rascal, isn't it wonderful to know that this is our home," I said, scratching him between the ears.

"What would be *really* wonderful," he yawned, "is if little kittens could get their beauty sleep without being disturbed ... or having their tails set alight like firecrackers."

He curled up into a ball and sighed.

"Oh, don't be grumpy!" I begged, stretching my arms and smiling as if it was Christmas morning all over again. That had been an amazing day, of course – with all the delicious food and exciting presents. But what I had now was far better than any present could ever be. I felt safe. I was part of a family – I had my beloved Rascal – and

I truly belonged here at last.

I had never felt like I belonged in the Magic Realm. I didn't fit in with all other young witches and wizards, and Aunt Hemlock was always so furious that I was hopeless at spells. The Ables didn't care what I was good at. They loved me for who I was.

A few days later, they proved that for sure.

It was the end of our first week back at school for the new term and our teacher, Miss Marker, gave us a spelling test. I usually do quite well, but this time I had forgotten to learn the list beforehand. It was full of really tricky Person World words like:

| | | |
|---|---|---|
| Refidgerator | ✗ | |
| Vacum Cleaner | ✗ | |
| Esculator | ✗ | |
| Elevater | ✗ | |
| Vaxination | ✗ | |
| Vechile | ✗ | |
| Aroplane | ✗ | |
| Bicicle | ✗ | |
| Carriage | ✓ | 1/10 |
| Yaught | ✗ | |

"One out of ten," tutted Miss Marker as she handed back my test. "What a pity, Bella. I know you can do much better than this."

"Slippery Serpents, that's terrible!" I groaned. I felt embarrassed and a bit nervous about telling Uncle Martin and Aunty Rose – they were always so pleased when I did well in tests and now they'd be disappointed in me, for sure. I was jiggling like a jellyfish by the time Aunty Rose came to pick me up at the end of school.

"Don't worry," said Esme kindly as we walked across the playground. "I'm sure you'll do better next time."

"I don't see what the problem is." Piers Seymour poked his head in between us. "I thought you were a witch, Bella? Why don't you just do a spell and change your score?

A *spelling* spell!" He giggled in delight at his own joke.

"Shh!" I hissed. "Someone will hear you. And anyway, I can't do any spells at the moment. I've sent my wand away for a whole month."

"It's true," whispered Esme. "She's given up magic for her New Year's resolution, just like I've given up sweets."

"Really?" Piers grinned and took a stripy paper bag out of his pocket – the sort you get from Merrymeet Sweet Shop. "I haven't given up anything!" he said as he popped a sugary lemon bonbon into his mouth. "I bet you're both sorry you did now."

"No! Not at all!" said Esme, but she was practically licking her lips as Piers waved the bag under her nose. He's much nicer than he used to be, but he still can't help being really annoying sometimes.

"I don't regret it either," I said truthfully. "Not one little bit." I did miss my wand, of course. But life in the Person World was so much simpler without magic. "And I would never have used a spell to change my score anyway. That's cheating."

"Ah! I didn't think cheating would bother a witch! I thought you're all supposed to be wicked?" Piers grinned.

"Sulking Salamanders! What a horrible thing to say."

"Sorry, Bella! I was only teasing." Piers looked genuinely guilty. I knew he didn't really mean any harm – he still just took things too far sometimes. But Esme wasn't going to let it rest that easily.

"Ignore him," she said, turning her back as he popped another lemon bonbon into his mouth. "He's only trying to wind us up. I shan't talk to him for the rest of the day!"

"Suit yourselves!" Piers shrugged and ran off with a cheeky grin. I had bigger things to worry about anyway. I could see Aunty Rose waving from the school gates. I would have to tell her about my test.

"What's the matter, pet?" she said, hurrying across the playground towards me. "You look worried."

"I've got something to show you," I mumbled, digging in my book bag and pulling out my spelling book. She was going to be so disappointed. The sooner I got it over with the better. "It's my spelling test. I only got one out of ten."

"Oh!" said Aunty Rose gently. "Well, that's not the end of the world, is it? From the look on your face, I thought something really bad had happened." She lifted my chin and smiled. "It's only a test. Uncle Martin and I will help you learn the spellings over the weekend and you can have another go on Monday."

"Really? That would be great!" I cried.

"All that ever matters to us is that you are happy, and you try your best," she said as the warm feeling came rushing back inside me – right down to the tips of my toes. And this time I wasn't snuggled up in my cosy bed with a kitten on my feet.

Aunty Rose hadn't shouted (like Aunt Hemlock used to every time I got a spell wrong), she hadn't screamed or sighed or even looked disappointed. She hadn't told me I was stupid and she certainly hadn't turned me into a slug as a punishment (which is probably what Aunt Hemlock would have done).

"Now, take that worried look off your face," she said brightly. "And let's go and see what all that fuss is by the gate." I looked over to where she was pointing and saw that there was a gaggle of excited parents and children gathered around the railings. They seemed to be looking at some sort of poster.

Before we had taken two steps, Esme came dashing back to tell us what it was all about.

"There's going to be a dance competition – like *Strictly Sequins*," she panted. "Only it's for children and it's going to be held right here in Merrymeet Village Hall."

"A dance contest!" Aunty Rose clapped her hands. "That *does* sound exciting. Will you both take part?"

"Of course we will!" said Esme. "Won't we, Bella?"

"Er..." I remembered my disastrous attempts at waltzing round the lounge with Uncle Martin. I glanced up at Aunty Rose.

I knew she wouldn't force me to take part. But she was looking so excited – and she loved the real *Strictly Sequins* show on tellyvision so much – how could I refuse? "Why not? I'll give it a go!" I said.

"That's the spirit!" cheered Aunty Rose. "Let's go and have a look at the poster, then."

I bit my lip as I followed Esme and Aunty Rose through the crowd. I knew it wasn't going to be easy. Especially without magic to help me. I could definitely learn to spell vacuum cleaner if I tried – but I wasn't sure I'd ever manage to dance a waltz!

# Chapter Seven

I held Esme's hand as she weaved through the excited crowd that had gathered by the school gates.

"Sorry!" I said. "Excuse me! Whoops! Sorry!" I must have stood on at least three Persons' toes on the way through. We squeezed past my friend Knox, the tallest boy in our class.

"Sorry, Knox! Can you see over our heads?" I asked as we ducked under his arm.

"No problem," he chuckled, towering above us.

We reached the front and saw the poster which had been hung on the railings. There was a picture of a huge sparkly glitter-ball trophy. The writing underneath it said:

MERRYMEET'S VERY OWN

STRICTLY SEQUINS

JUNIOR BALLROOM DANCING CONTEST

Beginners Welcome

Grand finals: Saturday 31ST January

At Merrymeet Village Hall

JUDGE: Ken Smyles from TV!

YES THAT'S RIGHT, KEN SMYLES FROM TV!!!

"The *real* Ken Smyles!" I gasped. "Just wait till Aunty Rose hears that he is going to be a judge." She was still at the back of the crowd, standing on tiptoe trying to see over the top of everybody's heads.

"And look," said Esme, pointing to a list of rules in smaller writing at the bottom of the poster. "It says there you have to be exactly our age to enter, which means it will probably be mostly other children from Indigo Class who take part."

"Thundering Falcons! It is exciting, isn't it?" I said. Who cares if I didn't know any proper ballroom dancing steps. It said beginners were welcome, and just taking part would be fun.

"All we need now is partners," said Esme.

"Partners?" I hadn't thought of that. But Esme was already squeezing back through the crowd.

"I'm going to find Piers," she called over her shoulder.

"But ... I thought you weren't speaking to him for the rest of the day," I said, tripping after her.

"Well, I am now!" said Esme as we reached the edge of the playground. "He might be annoying but his mum made him have ballroom dancing lessons last summer. They were on a fancy cruise ship or something. He's probably the best boy dancer in our class. Other than Zac ... and he'll be dancing with Zoe."

Esme was right. I could already see Zac and Zoe, the twins who sit on the same table as us in Indigo Class, dancing together round the climbing frame. They were only playing about at the moment, but their mum was a ballet teacher so they'd probably be really good.

"Piers!" cried Esme, spotting him by the climbing frame too. "I want to ask you something!"

"I thought you weren't talking to me?" Piers smirked.

Esme rolled her eyes. "I wish you still had your wand," she whispered to me. "Then you could make him disappear in a puff of smoke."

"But if I did that, you wouldn't have anyone to dance with!" I giggled.

"True! I suppose I'll just have to put up with him," said Esme, and she took a step forward, then suddenly stopped and turned back to me.

"Sorry, Bella – I didn't even ask," she whispered. "Do you want to see if Piers will be your partner instead? After all, you are neighbours."

"No," I said. "It's all right. You two will

be fantastic together." Esme might not have had ballroom dancing lessons but she had done ballet and tap. She was a brilliant performer. She deserved to have a good partner. And I knew Piers would be secretly pleased – although he'd probably make a huge fuss.

"So who will you dance with?" asked Esme, scratching her head.

"I don't know," I said, although I had been thinking exactly the same thing. "But if you want to ask Piers you better be quick." I could see Malinda – the meanest girl in Indigo Class – hurrying across the playground with her eyes on Piers like a goblin spying a pot of gold. Clearly word of his ballroom dancing lessons had got out.

"Thanks!" said Esme, and she dashed forward. "Piers, I need to talk to you."

Malinda stopped dead in her tracks,

scowled, and marched over to a quiet boy called Magnus. "You'll have to do!" I heard her say.

Malinda's friend Fay scuttled off towards a boy called Finn.

Everyone had stayed in the playground, buzzing with excitement. Best friends Keeley and Lexie were already trying to teach Paul and Akeem from their table to waltz. They both do gymnastics so would probably be pretty good at dancing too.

Everywhere I looked I realized children were asking each other to be partners. Most of the girls seemed excited. And plenty of the boys were too.

"It should be pretty cool. We might even get to be on telly," I heard Leo Austen, the most popular boy in the class, say. But a few of the other boys looked grumpy – or terrified. Some of them only agreed to take part when their mums or dads joined in to persuade them.

Aunty Rose smiled at me encouragingly across the playground. If I didn't pluck up courage and ask someone soon, there wouldn't be anybody left. As I didn't know much about ballroom dancing – or much about any sort of dancing, except how to spin around a cauldron or sway to a chant – I was hoping I might find someone pretty good. Someone who'd just let me follow their lead.

Aunty Rose was chatting to a boy called Cameron and his mum. I didn't know if he could dance, but he was pretty good at scoring goals, so maybe I should ask him.

*Football uses your feet and so does dancing*, I thought as I set off across the playground. *Cameron would probably make a great partner.*

But I had only taken two steps when I

saw that someone else didn't have a partner yet either.

Knox was hanging around by the gate, staring down at his big feet. He looked sad.

His tall and broad figure always reminded me a bit of a baby giant or a troll – I don't mean to be rude – back in the Magic Realm, a troll named Gawpaw is one of my best friends. Although Knox looks tough, he is just as kind and gentle as Gawpaw is – especially with animals. Rascal always loves it when he comes to our house; he tickles him under the chin for hours.

"Hi," I said, going over. "Aren't you going to dance with anyone?"

"I don't know." Knox shrugged. "I'd like to ... but I don't think anyone would want to be my partner. I'm a bit clumsy. Mum says I need to grow into these big flat feet of mine."

"Oh, Knox!" He wasn't exactly what I had in mind for an ideal partner, but he looked so miserable I couldn't bear it. "I'll dance with you," I said.

"Really?" He looked down at me and grinned.

"Of course." I said. "But Knox?"

"Yes?"

"Can you move?" I gulped. "Because you are standing on my toe!"

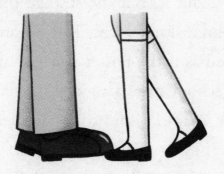

# Chapter Eight

News of Merrymeet's very own *Strictly Sequins* dance contest spread throughout the village like a whirlwind. Everyone was talking about it. But the strange thing was that nobody knew who had organized it. It seemed as if the poster had just appeared on the school gates that day.

"Like magic!" said our teacher, Miss Marker.

Piers and Esme both glanced at me. But

I shook my head. I didn't have anything to do with it. How could I? I didn't even have my wand.

Our head teacher didn't know anything about it either. And nor did Lady Trim, the chair of the village council.

Mrs Spinner, the ballet teacher, who was Zac and Zoe's mum, didn't know anything either. Although she did offer to give ballroom dancing lessons to small groups in the village hall.

"We're not having coaching from Mrs Spinner, are we, Esme?" boasted Piers, sticking his nose in the air as we walked home from school together the next day. "My parents are paying for us to have private lessons at the Big Bling Ballroom Academy in town."

"Yes..." Esme looked a bit embarrassed. Piers is always showing off about how much money his family has. Esme's mum has hardly any.

"The Academy does look gorgeous though," she whispered to me as we walked on. "I saw their website. There's a studio with mirrors all around the wall and a huge ballroom with a proper wooden dance floor as big as a car park."

"That's amazing," I said. I knew Esme would love having fancy lessons. She wants to be an actor or a dancer when she grows up. She would pick up the steps really quickly and be able to do a routine as complicated as any winning contestant on *Strictly Sequins*.

"I looked at the price though," she whispered. "I couldn't believe it. It costs an arm and a leg."

"Gulping Gargoyles!" I stopped dead in my tracks. "You have to give them an *arm and a leg* before they'll teach you to dance? That doesn't seem worth it."

"No!" Esme collapsed in fits of giggles. "It's just an expression. It means, it's really expensive."

"Oh!" I said, "Thank goodness for that. There was a horrid sorcerer in the Magic Realm who charged fingers to teach potions and spells."

"Yikes! In that case," said Esme, "I'm glad I might only have to learn to jive..."

We each had to pick a dance for the first round: jive, Argentine tango, waltz, cha-cha – there were so many to choose from.

I couldn't escape the *Strictly Sequins* madness when I got home either.

"What dance do you think you and Knox will do?" asked Aunty Rose as we ate supper that night.

"I don't know," I said, finding it a little hard to swallow my macaroni cheese. The idea of Knox and me standing up to dance in front of everyone we knew was suddenly terrifying. I didn't have a very good record when it came to performing in public. When we did a broomstick display in the Magic Realm, I landed head first in a pond.

I must have looked worried, because Uncle Martin cleared his throat and said, "You know what, Bella? If you want fancy lessons like Piers and Esme, I'm sure we can pay for a few."

"No," I said quickly. "Honestly, Knox and I will be fine." I didn't want Aunty Rose and Uncle Martin wasting their money. They weren't super-rich like Piers's parents, and no matter how many fancy classes I had, I was sure I would never dance as well as Esme. The sessions in the village hall would be fine for me.

"I'm really looking forward to being taught by Zac and Zoe's mum," I said truthfully. When I went round to their house for tea last term, she had been so graceful and pretty.

"I know Odette – I mean Mrs Spinner – usually teaches tap and ballet," said Aunty Rose. "But I bet she'll be brilliant at ballroom as well. And the most important thing is just to have fun."

"Exactly!" I agreed, feeling better already. And I took a big mouthful of macaroni cheese.

*Bella Broomstick, you are not going to be scared*, I told myself. *You are just going to* 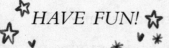 *HAVE FUN!*

"I am not going to be scared . . . I am going to have fun. I am not going to be scared . . . I am going to have fun," I chanted under my breath as I walked to the village hall on Saturday morning.

This was the Person World, after all. Nobody was going to turn me into a slimy frog if I got something wrong. My tummy felt as if it was full of little frogs though – all leaping about in there. I swallowed hard and waved to Knox, who was waiting outside the hall for me. He looked a little green in the face (a bit like a giant frog himself). Perhaps his tummy felt just as jumpy as mine.

"Do you know who we are having our sessions with?" I asked as he pushed open the door a little too fast and we nearly fell head first into the hall. Mrs Spinner had said she would take groups of three couples in each slot.

"Us!" said two friendly voices.

It was the twins.

"Brilliant!" I said. Other than Esme, I couldn't think of anyone I'd rather be with than Zac and Zoe. They wouldn't laugh no matter how hopeless poor Knox and I were.

"And us – not that we'd have chosen this group," said another far less friendly-sounding voice.

I looked towards the back of the hall and saw Malinda, the meanest girl in our whole class, standing there with her partner, Magnus.

My heart sank. If there was anyone who would laugh at us ... it was Malinda.

She stepped forward and curled her lip as she looked me and Knox up and down.

"Oh dear!" she sighed. "Couldn't you have made a little more of an effort?

Ballroom dancing is all about appearance, you know."

She did a little twirl to show off the custard-yellow cheerleader dress she was wearing with a big pink *M* on the front.

"I told Magnus he had to look smart too," she said, pointing to his dark trousers and crisp white shirt.

"Hi." Magnus blushed. I wasn't sure I'd ever heard him speak before – he's super shy. Although I remember he wrote a brilliant story once all about what it would be like to fly on a magic carpet at night. Miss Marker read it out for him in class – he got the feeling of soaring amongst the stars absolutely right.

"Hi," I said, noticing the twins had started stretching and warming up now. They had proper dance leotards in gold and black.

"I hadn't realized we were meant to wear something special," I said. I was in my favourite, comfy dungarees and a stripy T-shirt. Knox was wearing his football kit, with long stripy socks, his knobbly knees poking out underneath his shorts.

"It doesn't matter at all. As long as you are comfy," said Zoe kindly.

Malinda sighed. "Excuse me. I've got a lot of work to do." She took a deep breath, raised her arms over her head, then spun past us in a series of dazzling cartwheels, showing off the custard-yellow knickers that matched her cheerleader dress.

"I just hope you two aren't going to hold the rest of us back, that's all," she said, tossing her ponytail as she landed in the splits.

# Chapter Nine

"One, two, three. One, two, three..." Mrs Spinner clapped her hands as Knox and I attempted to move our feet in time to the beat. "Brilliant." She beamed. "That is so much better."

"I know!" Knox beamed too. "I only trod on Bella's toes once that time."

"Yes!" I tried to smile cheerfully. I didn't want to make Knox feel bad, but my eyes were watering and I was limping slightly.

Unfortunately, the "once" that he had trodden on me was quite hard ... more of a stamp than a step really. My poor feet were going to be black and blue by tonight.

"Just keep practising," said Mrs Spinner, heading back across the hall to work with Malinda and Magnus. "One, two, three. One, two, three... If you can master that beat, then you can waltz!"

"One, two, three. One, two, three... Whoops!" said Knox and I, banging into each other like two blind bats in a dark cave.

I heard Malinda sniggering behind our backs, but I ignored her. She had already told us our waltz was easy-peasy. She and Magnus were doing a really fast jive. And the twins were practising a Charleston with so many lifts and turns it made my head spin.

"Right – I mean ... left!" I said as Knox

and I shuffled across the floor. "Let's try again. One, two, three. One, two, three."

How do the dancers on *Strictly Sequins* make it look so easy?

I think poor Knox was even worse than I was. He made Uncle Martin seem like a king of the dance floor.

"Sorry," he said, bumping into me again. But I couldn't be cross. He was so apologetic and we were both trying our very best.

Then, just before the end of the session, we managed to get round the floor once without treading on each other's toes at all.

"Spinning Spiders! That was fun!" I whooped.

"We did it!" roared Knox.

"Well done," said Magnus shyly.

"Yeah, whatever!" said Malinda, curling her lip. "It's not like you're going to win the Glitter-Ball Trophy or anything."

Mrs Spinner shot her a surprised look. "Knox and Bella have made great progress today. But you've all got a lot of work to do," she said firmly. "The knockout round is next Saturday. . ."

"Knockout round!" Knox groaned. "Does that mean we have to dance twice?"

"Only if you're good enough to get through," said Malinda with a nasty little laugh. "Which – let's face it – you're not!"

"That's quite enough!" Mrs Spinner shot her another stern look. "As I was saying, the knockout round is next Saturday. That's when the judges decide who will get to dance in the Grand Final the week after. Only three couples will go through, so you all need to dance the very best that you can."

Then she dismissed the class and we gathered up our things.

Malinda's dad, Mr Victor, was standing in the corridor, wagging his finger at his daughter as we squeezed past.

"I was watching you through the window, Malinda," I heard him say. "Some of those turns were far too slow. And your footwork was sloppy. You'll have to work much harder than that if you want a place in the final."

"Poor Malinda," I whispered to Knox when we were outside. "No wonder she's so mean sometimes if her parents are as tough on her as that."

"Exactly." Knox frowned. "At least our parents don't mind how we do." Then he smiled. "I'm sorry, Bella, but I don't think we're going to make it to the final. Do you?"

"No!" I agreed as we banged into each other trying to get out of the gate. No matter what her dad said, Malinda and Magnus were already far better than we were. So were the twins. I was pretty sure they would be two of the three couples in the final at least. Then there was Esme and Piers. They'd be brilliant. And a few others were having fancy dance lessons in town too.

"I'll just be happy if we don't fall over," I said, pretending to waltz away down the lane.

"Ark! Ark!" I jumped back in surprise as the horrid magpie appeared out of nowhere. It swooped down and began to circle around my head. "Ark! Ark!"

It was as if it was laughing at what I had just said.

"Shoo!" Knox waved his arms and the

bird flew off on to the roof of the village hall.

"Horrible thing. I keep seeing it everywhere," I said, hurrying down the lane to get away. My heart was pounding again. I don't know why I was so frightened of that silly bird. Maybe it's because it wouldn't talk to me properly in its own language. I usually love all animals. Aunt Hemlock's cave was full of rats and bats and spiders. All sorts of creepy crawlies too. But I wasn't scared of any of them. I would chat to them for hours. They were my friends.

"Are you wearing a shiny hair clip or something?" asked Knox, catching up with me as I fled along the pavement. "I know magpies love anything that glitters or shines. It might have been trying to steal that."

"No," I said, slowing down and patting my head. I do have a shiny hair clip. It's shaped like a star. But I wasn't wearing it today. I didn't like to say to Knox that I thought the magpie had been following me for weeks. Ever since New Year's Day, in fact.

"Come on," I said, trying to walk normally as I glanced over my shoulder and the magpie hopped on to a letter box. "It's only a silly bird. Let's go."

Knox was coming home with me so Aunty Rose could measure him. His mum is a busy nurse and she was working long shifts at the hospital all week, so Aunty Rose had offered to make dance outfits for both of us.

"Mum hates sewing," said Knox. "It was such a relief not to have to worry about it."

"Aunty Rose loves it. She's really excited," I said. "And now we know we're dancing a waltz, we can all decide what she should make."

Knox scratched his head. "I don't really have a clue."

"Don't worry." I shrugged. "Nor do I. But if Aunty Rose has anything to do with it, there'll be sequins galore!"

"Sequins? They'll be really shiny! Better make sure that magpie doesn't see you when you're wearing your sparkly costume," said Knox. "It might try and steal you and take you back to its nest!"

"Oh, don't say that!" I cried, even though I knew he was only joking.

"Ark! Ark!" laughed the magpie from a tree . . . and it followed us all the way home.

# Chapter Ten

The dress that Aunty Rose made for me was amazing. It was a gorgeous pink colour like my flamingo pen and covered in shimmering sequins. She made Knox a pair of glittery trousers and a sequin waistcoat too.

I helped sew on sequins for a whole afternoon and evening. I don't know how Aunty Rose has the patience. Sometimes the Person World is such hard work. I'd have given anything to have my wand with me. I would have sneakily waved it when Aunty Rose wasn't looking:

*Sequins, sew yourselves on tight*
*Make this dress sparkle bright!*

I was counting the days till I could call my flamingo back home. I'd put a tiny pencil cross on Aunty Rose's calendar:

Sunday 1st February. The day after the Grand Final of the *Strictly Merrymeet* dance contest, I would go to the top of the hill and call for her. Then, if I was *very careful*, perhaps I could go back to using a few tiny, secret spells to help with those Person World chores that take hours when you have to do them without magic – like changing my duvet cover and sorting socks.

Meanwhile, there was nothing else for it but to thread my needle again, and help to sew on the last few sequins by hand. But it was worth it in the end.

"It's beautiful," said Esme when she came round to our house to see the dress.

She was dancing a complicated Viennese waltz with Piers, which had lots of lifts and spins. Mrs Seymour had ordered her a special gold gown with matching shoes from a shop in London and insisted on paying for it all.

"But I think your dress is even prettier," Esme said. "And it's so much nicer to have one that's home-made."

"I wish I could see you and Piers dance," I said.

But Esme shook her head. "Not until tomorrow night, at the knockout round. I promised I'd keep it secret until then," she said. "I'm not even supposed to say what dance we're doing, and I *definitely* shouldn't have told you about the dress."

"Don't worry," I said. "My lips are sealed. But I think everyone in Merrymeet knows what Knox and I are doing."

We had been so desperate to improve, we had practised in the playground every day at break.

"You'll be great!" said Esme.

"Of course she will!" agreed Aunty Rose,

popping her head around the door. "And anyway..."

"*It's only a bit of fun!*" we all chorused together.

"Now," said Aunty Rose, "are you girls coming to help decorate the village hall?"

"Yes!" I said. If I was honest, I was looking forward to the decorating tonight, even more than the dancing tomorrow.

"The theme is sequins and stars," said Mrs Spinner, when we had all gathered in the hall. "We thought we'd hang up as many sparkly things as we possibly can. And Lady Trim from the council has hired a giant disco ball."

"Sounds wicked!" Esme whistled through her teeth.

"Why?" I said, grabbing her sleeve and pulling her anxiously to one side. "What's *wicked* about a disco ball? Is it evil?"

"Don't look so worried. It's just another expression." Esme laughed. "*Wicked* actually means something's going to be really good!"

"But that doesn't make any sense," I said. "There's nothing good at all about being wicked!"

"I suppose not!" Esme nodded. She had met Aunt Hemlock face-to-face, after all. "Let's say it's going to be ... sequin-spectacular instead!"

"Sequin-spectacular!" I agreed, taking one end of a shimmering string of silver tinsel and helping her hang it around the old piano at the side of the stage.

Then we helped tie silver ribbons around the chairs and hung glittery streamers from the ceiling.

By the time we were finished, the village

hall was covered from floor to rafters in twinkling tinsel, shimmering stars and sparkly sequins.

"Flickering Fairies, it's so pretty!" I gasped. I am always amazed at how beautiful Persons can make things look without magic to help them. Even with my flamingo wand and the sparkliest spell in the world, I don't think I could have done a better job than we all did with only sticky tape and drawing pins to help us. Esme and I lay on our backs in the middle of the stage, staring up at the ceiling. I felt as if we might be lying on a far-off planet, looking up at an enchanted sky.

"Thank you all for working so hard," said Lady Trim from the council.

"Three cheers for Merrymeet!" bellowed Uncle Martin.

"Hip, hip, hooray!" we all roared.

Then Mrs Spinner looked at her watch.

"Goodness me, it's nearly midnight," she gasped, bustling the twins towards the door. "It's a good job it's not a school night. At least you can all have a lie-in before the knockout round tomorrow night."

Everyone began to hurry home.

We were the last to leave, as Uncle Martin offered to lock up and put all the ladders and tools away.

As we stepped out of the door at last, the street was deserted.

Bong! Bong! Bong. . . The clock on the church tower began to chime.

"Midnight!" whispered Aunty Rose. "They call it the witching hour!"

I shivered even though I was wrapped up warm in my bright red Christmas coat.

"Look!" Uncle Martin called us back

over to the big window in the front of the village hall. "Someone has put the trophy on display."

Sure enough, a sparkling glitter-ball trophy, like the one we had seen on the poster, was shining in the window.

"Funny. I wonder who put it there?" said Uncle Martin, scratching his head. "There was no one in the hall when I locked up. I checked the whole place three times."

"It must have been Lady Trim before she left," said Aunty Rose, linking arms with us both as she bustled us down the street. "Time for bed."

But I glanced back over my shoulder as the shiny trophy shone in the window like a star.

It was same as the poster for the competition. It seemed as if the glitter-ball trophy had appeared out of nowhere.

Almost like magic.

# Chapter Eleven

The next day sped by in a whirl of preparation for the knockout round that night.

Knox and I had a last-minute rehearsal with Mrs Spinner in the hall. And Esme and Piers were away all day at the fancy dance studio in town.

Aunty Rose wanted to alter the hem on my costume. And, then, before I knew it, it was almost time to go.

I stood in front of the bathroom mirror for a moment, staring at myself in the beautiful sparkly dress. I couldn't believe it was really me ... I looked like a princess from a fairy tale.

"And I thought you were supposed to be a wicked witch," I whispered to my reflection with a smile. (The mirror didn't answer me, of course. They never do in the Person World.)

Then I came downstairs and Uncle Martin pretended to faint.

"What? No dungarees today?" he said with a cheeky grin. "I'd better give us all a lift to the village hall. I don't want you getting mud on that beautiful frock."

As we parked the car, we saw crowds had already started to gather.

Some were still outside the hall, peering in the window at the Glitter-Ball Trophy.

I could see Malinda's parents pushing her to the very front.

"That's what it's all about. Getting through to the Grand Final, so you can win that trophy next week," I heard her father say.

Others were already inside.

"Let's go and get a good seat," said Uncle Martin.

We squeezed through groups of gossiping parents as we made our way across the hall.

I could see Mrs Lee at the front with Esme's little sister, Gretel.

"Martin! Rose! I've saved you a place in the front row," she beamed.

Then suddenly a whisper ran round the hall and I saw heads craning towards the back of the room.

"Ken Smyles is here!"

"Ooooh! Ken Smyles. I can't wait to see

him in real life!" Aunty Rose clapped her hands with excitement.

"Over here, Mr Smyles!" A skinny photographer from the local paper dashed across the room. "The *Merrymeet Mercury*... Can I have a BIG *smile*, Mr Smyles?"

A hush fell over the hall.

The crowd parted, then all the parents began to clap and cheer as Ken Smyles scuttled towards the judges' table at the front of the room.

He was much smaller than I had expected. As he passed right in front of me, he stopped and grinned. It wasn't the famous shiny-toothed smile I'd seen on telly-vision or on Aunty Rose's calendar. Close up, his teeth looked rather small and sharp.

He looked up at me for a moment and licked his lips as if they were dry. I saw his orangey skin was leathery and cracked.

"Well, well, well! What a sparkly dress. Good luck, *Bella*!" he said. Then he scurried on and the crowd closed in behind him.

It was only after he'd gone that I realized how strange it was that he'd known my name.

"Mr Smyles? Wait!" I cried. But it was no good, the crowd was surging forward to get a better look at the famous telly-vision star. There was no way I could squeeze through in my delicate, sequin waltzing dress, and anyway he had reached the stage by now.

"Ladies and gentlemen, boys and girls, good evening. Thank you for having me. Such an honour. Such an honour to be here in Merryfeet – I mean Merrymeet," He grinned and licked his cracked, dry lips again. "Yes. Such an honour."

"Bella!" I saw Esme beckoning to me from the little door at the front of the hall, which led behind the curtains backstage. Her golden gown sparkled as if it was made of a thousand twinkling stars – like something an enchanted a wood nymph would wear.

"You look amazing!" I cried.

"So do you!" She grinned. "But we're not supposed to be out the front here in our costumes. You better come through, quick."

"Oh! I didn't realize." I waved goodbye to Uncle Martin and Aunty Rose.

"Good luck!" called Aunty Rose.

"Break a leg!" hollered Uncle Martin. (I was quite surprised – why would he tell me to do that? – but Esme explained it was just something Persons say before you go on stage. It didn't seem to make any sense at all!)

Backstage, everyone looked wonderful in their glittering costumes. I had never seen so many sequins and sparkles and ruffles and frills.

As soon as all the couples had arrived, Mrs Spinner stood up on a chair and clapped her hands.

"Quiet, please, everybody. The contest will start in five minutes," she said. "I want absolute silence backstage while the dancing is going on. When you have finished your own performance, please don't come back here to the dressing room. Leave the stage on the left-hand side and follow the stairs up to the balcony. You'll be able to watch the rest of the show from up there."

"Yes, miss," we all mumbled.

Mrs Spinner pinned a piece of paper to

the curtain. "This is the order you will dance in," she explained. "Make sure you are ready to come out on to the stage as soon as the couple before you have left. Piers and Esme, you are first. So stand here by the entrance. Then Keeley and Paul behind them. That's it. Then Lexie and Akeem. Finn and Fay..."

I listened, my knees shaking, as Mrs Spinner read on through the list. I wished I could stand close to Esme and Piers, but more and more names were read out and Knox and I had still not been called to line up.

"... Then Zac and Zoe," continued Mrs Spinner. She was nearly at the very bottom of her list. "And, right at the end here – last but not least – Bella and Knox."

"We're the last to dance?" I gasped. I didn't know if I could bear to wait that long. My knees were wobbling like a skeleton on a sleigh. I heard Knox gulp nervously beside me and gave his hand a reassuring squeeze. At least we were in this together.

But all I wanted to do was run away...

# Chapter Twelve

There was a thundering round of applause as Esme and Piers stepped onstage to open the show.

"Look!" whispered Zac. "There's a slit in the curtains. If we peep out, we can watch them dance."

Zac, Zoe and I bunched up together to spy through the gap. Knox peered over the top of my head.

Mr Spinner, the twins' dad, was sitting

just in front of us at the sound desk on the
edge of the stage. He had all our pieces
of music lined up on the computer ready
to play. As the crowd fell silent, he tapped
the keyboard and the tune of the Viennese
waltz that Esme and Piers had chosen filled
the hall.

I thought Piers might be silly and giggly
but he was clearly taking it very seriously –
he took Esme in his arms and they began

to twirl across the stage together in perfect unison. They spun as smoothly as if they were parchment in the wind. All those fancy dance lessons had been worth every single penny the Seymours had spent. I forgot that they were two ordinary children from Indigo Class. Or that Piers usually spent most of his time trying to put spiders in Esme's lunchbox. They were like Prince Charming and Cinderella at a ball.

As the music died away, they froze for a moment at the end of their dance and the audience went wild. Through the curtain, I could see Esme's mum and Gretel in the front row. Gretel was so excited she was standing on her chair. Uncle Martin leapt to his feet and cheered. Aunty Rose joined him and Piers's proud parents stood up too. Soon the whole audience were on their feet.

"Well done, Esme!" I heard Aunty Rose shout.

Lady Trim held up her scorecard first:

Then the second judge, Miss Swan, who had once been a famous ballet dancer, and lived in a pretty white cottage behind the church, held up hers: 10.

Then Ken Smyles: 8.

A few of the audience booed at the last score.

"They should have got straight tens!" whispered Zoe.

But it was an amazing score overall. I was so proud — they would go through to the Grand Final next week for sure.

Piers bowed and Esme curtsied before they dashed offstage and disappeared up to the balcony.

I wished I could have been up there with them. That would mean our dance was over too and we had nothing left to do except relax and watch everyone else perform. Keeley and Paul were already starting their rumba. Right after them it was Lexie and Akeem, who were trying a tango ... There were a few slips and wobbles but everyone was doing brilliantly. On and on the couples danced, getting closer and closer to my turn with Knox.

Suddenly the whole audience gasped.

Poor Malinda had flung her leg so high she kicked Magnus right under the chin.

Bam!

He fell backwards on to the floor and landed on his bottom. Hard.

"Ouch! Whoops! Sorry!" He blushed as he scrambled to his feet and tried to finish the dance. But they were all out of time with the music by now.

I could see Malinda's furious parents scowling at her from the audience. Her father even wagged his finger at her from his seat.

"Poor thing," I whispered. I know she had been mean to me – and especially to Knox – but I thought how horrible it must be to have parents who pushed her so hard and only seemed to care about whether she would get a place in the Grand Final and win the Glitter-Ball Trophy next week. No

wonder Malinda was always so snappy —
inside she must feel like she had a nervous
tummy full of crocs.

Now she had no chance of getting to the
Grand Final. Nobody had come close to
Esme and Piers's high score yet, but plenty
of dances had scored sevens and eights.

Malinda left the stage in tears as poor
blushing Magnus scurried up the stairs to
the balcony after her, rubbing his chin.

"Idiot!" she hissed. Although it wasn't
his fault.

"Trembling Turtles!" I gulped. If I had
been nervous before, watching Malinda and
Magnus made it far worse. They were much
better dancers than Knox and I. If things
had gone so terribly wrong for them, how
could we stand a chance?

"Oh no! It's nearly us!" I heard Knox
groan beside me as the twins got ready to

walk out onstage.

"Good luck!" We waved to Zac and Zoe.

They had the crowd captivated from the moment they took their first step to the music. They were brilliant and so smooth and fast – even better than they had been in rehearsal. Their jaunty Charleston made the audience clap along in time to the beat and laugh out loud as Zac and Zoe shimmied across the stage with huge jolly grins on their faces. It was slick and fun and they were clearly loving every moment.

Then it was over. The twins were finished. The crowd were on their feet again.

Lady Trim held up her card: 10.

Miss Swan: 10.

Ken Smyles: 8.

The same score as Esme and Piers. And, once again, Ken Smyles was the only judge who had been mean. But it meant they would be in the Grand Final too.

Zoe curtsied. Zac bowed. Then they ran up the stairs to the balcony where the rest of the class were waiting.

"Ready, Knox?" I gulped. It was our turn now. There was nowhere to hide.

"Good luck, Bella!" he mumbled as we stepped forward. At least, I think that's what he said – it was more of a terrified choking sound than actual words.

"Good luck, Knox!" I whispered. But my stomach felt like a bubbling cauldron. Then we stepped through the curtain and on to the stage.

# Chapter Thirteen

Knox and I stood facing each other on the stage, or knees shaking as we waited for our waltz music to begin.

We waited.

And waited...

The audience began to shuffle.

Somebody laughed.

I glanced over at Mr Spinner on the sound desk.

"Sorry!" he mouthed. "Bit of a problem with the music."

We waited a little more.

I glanced at the audience. Aunty Rose and Uncle Martin were smiling encouragingly. "I am so sorry, ladies and gentlemen." Mr Spinner stood up from his desk. "Bit of a technical hitch! There may be a short delay. Knox and Bella's music seems to have vanished."

"Vanished?" said Ken Smyles from the judges' table. "How very odd." He was still licking his lips in that strange way I had never noticed him do on telly-vision. He reminded me a bit of a newt.

Mr Spinner looked at us apologetically. "I can't find your tune anywhere on the computer," he said. "I even did spare copy of all the tracks before the show and that's gone too."

"No hurry," said Miss Swan kindly from the judges' table. "We can wait."

Mr Spinner bent over the computer again, his forehead creased with concentration. "Perhaps I can help," said a thin, crackly voice from the back of the hall. There was a shuffle of movement and an old woman with a black cloak over her head began to hobble up the aisle.

"I shall play the music for you," she said. "It is *The Midnight Waltz*, yes?"

"Yes!" cried Mr Spinner enthusiastically. "Do you know the tune?"

"I do!" the old woman wheezed.

I had never thought about the name of the music before: *The Midnight Waltz* – like the witching hour. I shuddered. The old lady had reached the stage by now. She nodded to Knox, then turned her head towards me and looked straight into my eyes.

"Hello, my dear!" she said.

She had disguised herself, of course. But I would recognize that cold, dark stare anywhere.

"Aunt Hemlock!" I gasped.

"Shh!" She put a thin finger to her lips. "Don't worry, I am here to help."

"*Help?*" That couldn't be true. Aunt Hemlock had never helped me in her whole life.

"Do you know her?" whispered Knox.

"Erm. . ." I shook my head. How could I explain who she really was when I was standing onstage in front of every Person in the whole of Merrymeet. I couldn't just say: "Let me introduce you all to my aunt Hemlock. She's a wicked witch who's come all the way from the Magic Realm."

"Shall we begin?" Aunt Hemlock brushed

past me and I felt goosebumps on my arm. She shuffled over to the old piano which had been pushed against the wall at the side of the stage.

"I shall play this old magpie box," she said, lifting the lid on the piano and running her long, bony fingers along the black-and-white keys.

"The magpie box?" Mr Spinner laughed. "I've never heard a piano called that before. But thank you."

I stared at Aunt Hemlock in her little-old-lady disguise – black cloak, long white hair – like a magpie herself. "Dusty Demons!" I gasped. "Of course!" That's why the bird had unsettled me so much. It had been Aunt Hemlock in yet another cunning disguise. She had been spying on me in the village all this time.

The audience had begun to clap and

cheer, excited that they would get to see our dance at last.

All I knew was that something terrible was bound to happen the minute Aunt Hemlock began to play.

She would have to use magic. She couldn't really play the piano at all. There are no pianos in the Magic Realm. No real music, except the tin flutes the trolls make or the rattling bones the spooks and skeletons play.

"One, two, three," said Aunt Hemlock, stretching her fingers above the keys as a hush fell over the room.

She hunched low over the piano and I saw her shoulders move as if she was muttering an incantation.

Pom!

Perfect! There it was – the first note of *The Midnight Waltz.*

Pom! Pom! ♫

Without knowing how, my feet began to move.

*It's enchanted music,* I thought, swaying to the rhythm. If I was under the spell of her playing, Aunt Hemlock could make me do anything she wanted. She could make me fall flat on my face...

I waited to stumble...

But I did not fall. And nor did Knox. We both began to float across the floor ... I mean almost literally float. Our feet barely seemed to touch the ground at all.

Big, broad Knox moved with the grace and elegance of a fairy king.

"Wow!" he whispered in my ear as he spun me around. "We're doing really well, Bella. We've never danced as brilliantly as this before. We're amazing!"

"We are," I said, and, in spite of

everything, I almost began to enjoy myself. It was wonderful to be so feather-light and free. I felt, if I stretched my arms, I might fly away, right up amongst the sparkly sequin stars on the ceiling.

We were spinning and spinning and spinning. . .

Then, with a final flourish, it was over. Knox and I floated to a halt and the audience were up on their feet.

Aunty Rose had tears streaming down her face. "Well done!" she cried.

"Bravo!" Uncle Martin opened and closed his mouth in surprise. "Bravo!"

I glanced towards Aunt Hemlock at the piano. She smiled and gave a little bow. My knees went weak and I had to clutch hold of Knox for a moment to stop myself falling over. What was happening? Aunt Hemlock had used magic tonight, that

was for sure. But she had used it to *help* me. She had never done anything like that ever before. In the past, she was always turning me into a slug or punishing me with a terrible dose of itchy toad pox. But now her enchanted music had made Knox and me dance brilliantly. I knew it was wrong. She shouldn't have used magic to help us. But I had to admit, it felt wonderful. As if we had been made of air.

The judges held up their cards.

Lady Trim: 10

Miss Swan: 10

Ken Smyles grinned and licked his lips. And suddenly I knew – it wasn't a newt he reminded me of, it was a lizard. The leathery skin, the small sharp teeth where there should have been a big broad smile...

This wasn't the real Ken Smyles from

telly-vision. It was Wane, Aunt Hemlock's shape-shifting chameleon in disguise.

"Congratulations!" he said, turning his scorecard over: 10.

"It's a ten from Ken!" He winked.

Lady Trim stood up as the audience clapped again. "That's the knockout round over!" she shouted over the noise. "The three couples going through to next week's Grand Final will be Esme Lee and Piers Seymour, Zac and Zoe Spinner and finally, with the highest score of the night, Knox Bailey and Bella Broomstick."

"Well done, all of you," said Miss Swan.

"But only one lucky couple will win the magnificent Glitter-Ball Trophy!" said Wane in his Ken Smyles disguise. He licked his lips as if he was waiting to catch a fly.

My head was spinning.

I looked over my shoulder and saw Aunt

Hemlock disappearing up the aisle, her black cloak flapping behind her like wings. She gave me a little wave, then slipped out the door and away into the night. That was it! She was gone. She didn't try and take me with her. She didn't threaten me ... or turn me into a frog. Nothing! Had she really just come here to help?

"Esme and Piers, come on down." Lady Trim beckoned them from the balcony. "And Zac and Zoe too. Let's have all the finalists onstage."

The twins came first, grinning from ear to ear. Piers and Esme followed. But neither of them were smiling. Esme's face was as dark as thunder and Piers stuck his tongue out at me as he took a bow.

"I knew I couldn't trust you!" he hissed in my ear, while Esme turned to the audience and curtsied. It was only when she came and stood next to me that I saw her eyes were full of tears.

"How could you, Bella?" she whispered. "You ruined other people's chances. You used magic to get into the final. That's cheating. It's not fair!"

# Chapter Fourteen

I tried to catch up with Piers and Esme backstage after the show. I could understand why they were so furious, but I had to try and explain what had happened.

Piers put his hands on his hips and scowled at me across the room.

"Cheat!" he mouthed.

But Esme just grabbed her coat and stormed off.

"Leave me alone. I don't want to talk to you," she said.

I charged after her through the hall, still wearing my fancy ball gown, ignoring shouts of congratulations as I weaved through the crowd. "I won't be a minute," I called to Uncle Martin and Aunty Rose as I ran outside.

"Esme, wait!" I caught up with her on the path. "You have to listen to me," I said, leading her over to a bench. I looked around to check no one else could hear us.

"You're right," I whispered. "It was magic that made Knox and me dance so well. But it wasn't me who did it. It can't have been. You know it can't. I don't even have my wand."

Esme shrugged. "If it wasn't you, who was it then?"

"Aunt Hemlock," I said. "You saw her. She was playing the piano."

"All I saw was an old woman in a cloak," said Esme. "Cameron said it was Mrs Allen. She used to teach piano to his big sister but she's retired now. And Fay thought it was Miss Button, who used to play campfire songs when her cousin was in the Brownies."

"You see," I said. "Nobody knows for sure who she was. It was Aunt Hemlock in disguise. And as for Ken Smyles, that was Wane."

"Wane, the chameleon?" Esme raised her eyebrows. "So what are you saying? Ken Smyles, the famous TV host of *Strictly Sequins*, is a *lizard*?"

"Yes!" I said. "I mean, no. Not the real one. But the judge who was here tonight. That was Wane. He's a shape-shifter, he can disguise himself as almost anything he wants."

"OK," said Esme slowly. "So you are saying Wane and Aunt Hemlock came all the way from the Magic Realm to help you get through to the final of the *Strictly Merrymeet* ballroom dancing contest?"

I thought for a minute — remembering the mysterious poster that appeared from nowhere and the magpie that had been following me ever since. "No," I said slowly. "I think Aunt Hemlock was the one who planned the whole thing in the first place. I think she put the posters up on the school gate," I said.

"I see," said Esme. "She planned the whole thing?"

"Yes!" I cried, relieved that Esme seemed to be understanding me at last. I took a step forward to give her a hug. But she pushed my arms away.

Esme shook her head. "Why would Aunt

Hemlock plan a lovely glittery dance contest and then use her magic to help you get to the Grand Final? It doesn't make any sense, Bella." Her voice softened a little. "Aunt Hemlock never does anything to help you. She hates you... You've said so yourself, a billion times. So why would she use her magic to help you now?"

"I don't know." Tears sprang to the corner of my eyes. "I'm as confused as you are, Esme."

"I'm sorry, Bella. I want to believe you, but I can't. You must have used your own magic tonight. Perhaps you gave up on your New Year's resolution and got your wand back somehow..." She looked at her shoes for a moment. "I haven't been perfect on mine either. I had two toffees when we were in Piers's car." She pulled the wrappers out of her coat pocket. "Perhaps you were trying to be kind," she said. "Maybe you did it so that people wouldn't laugh at Knox. But it was still wrong. The twins and Piers and I all worked really hard to win our place in the Grand Final. We didn't have any magic to help us. And you ruined the chance for other people – everyone in the class worked hard – they would have all loved the chance to dance again next week. Everyone wants to win that trophy, Bella."

"This isn't fair!" I grabbed her sleeve. "You're my best friend." She still looked so furious, I felt as if my heart would break. "Why won't you trust me?"

"Why should I trust you?" she snapped. "You're a witch."

"Esme?" I stumbled backwards, as if she had slapped me in the face.

She looked shocked too. A tear ran down her cheek.

"I've got to go," she said, leaping to her feet and running away. "I've got to find my mum, or we'll miss the bus."

I sat alone for a long time after Esme was gone. She was right to be angry – it wasn't fair that Knox and I had got through to the final thanks to magic. But it wasn't my fault. No matter what Esme thought, I didn't do the spell myself. And I certainly did not invite Aunt Hemlock to do it for it for me.

So what was going on? Why had she come to Merrymeet to help me out? And if she really had planned the whole dance contest in the first place – then why?

I began to pace up and down, but it was no good, I couldn't get any answers.

I was still pacing when Aunty Rose and

Uncle Martin came to find me.

"There you are!" said Uncle Martin, wrapping his warm scarf around my shoulders. "You look worn out. I'm not surprised after the way you danced. Congratulations on getting through to the Grand Final!"

"I'm so proud of you, Bella," beamed Aunty Rose, kissing the top of my head. "Thank you," I mumbled. I wanted to tell them not to be proud of me – that I shouldn't be in the final – that I had only gone through because of magic. But I couldn't. Especially not as the hall began to empty and a big gaggle of parents and children all spilled out on to the path at once.

Knox came over with his mum, and the twins ran up and patted us both on the back.

"Well done! You were amazing," Zac beamed.

"I'm so pleased we're all going to be in the Grand Final together," said Zoe.

"Amazing!" agreed Knox. No one was more surprised – or pleased – than him. "I – I don't know how we did it. It just didn't feel real, did it, Bella?"

"No," I said quietly. How could I ever tell him that it *wasn't* real, that he hadn't actually danced that well at all? It was just a spell.

"You certainly saved your best performance for when it mattered," said Mrs Spinner. "Quite extraordinary. Well done, both of you."

"Thank you!" I said, and Knox bowed as he waltzed away down the path with his mum.

"Ouch!" she squealed as he trod on her toes.

It was clear Aunt Hemlock's magic had

worn off already. And that's when it hit me.

No matter what had happened here tonight, it wasn't over yet ... we would still have to dance again in the Grand Final. No matter how thrilling the performance had been, I didn't want Aunt Hemlock to come back and help us next time – Esme was right. It was cheating. It wasn't fair on anybody else. And, whatever her reasons for coming to our rescue, Aunt Hemlock wouldn't be doing all this for nothing.

If she did come back for the final next Saturday, she would be bound to want something in return. But what would it be?

# Chapter Fifteen

Esme sat next to me as usual for our lessons at school, but she barely spoke to me at break times for the whole of the next week. It broke my heart. She wasn't mean or unkind, she just always made sure there was someone else around so that we were never alone together.

"I don't want to talk about it," she said the one time I did manage to get her on her own and tried to explain to her again that the magic wasn't my fault.

Meanwhile Piers was being really horrid. He kept sticking his tongue out and whispering to other children in corners. Perhaps I had been wrong to trust him with my secret at all. No matter how cross with me she was, I knew Esme would never tell anyone I was a witch. But Piers might announce it to the whole village for all I knew. He was just as cross as Esme that magic had won Knox and me our place in the final.

"My parents are paying for more expensive dance lessons for me and Esme. We're doing the paso doble in the Grand Final," he told me over the garden wall on the day after the knockout round. "But it's probably all a BIG waste of money – because you're just going to wave a wand to win anyway."

"That's not true!" I said. "It wasn't me who used magic. You know I can't get my wand back until the beginning of February. That's not until next Sunday. The final will be over by then."

"Whatever!" Piers shrugged. I could tell he didn't believe me.

But before I could say anything else, Uncle Martin came into the garden to feed his birds. Piers stuck his tongue out at me for the hundredth time and went back inside his house.

Uncle Martin didn't see anything. He whistled as he pretended to waltz from one feeder to another. At least he seemed genuinely pleased for me. And Aunty Rose was thrilled too. She couldn't wait to get started on the new costumes which Knox and I would wear in the Grand Final.

The twins had chosen a tango right away ... but Knox and I weren't sure what routine we should do. I was too busy trying to think of ways to get out of the whole thing.

"If it's any help, I found this note pinned to the door," said Mrs Spinner when we turned up to our first rehearsal on Monday morning before school. We were going to have to practise every minute that we could, as there was only a week to prepare for the Grand Final.

"The note must be from the old lady who played the piano for you," said Mrs Spinner. "But it's not signed." She unfolded a piece of yellowy paper and showed us a scribbled message in green ink. I would have recognized Aunt Hemlock's spiky handwriting anywhere:

I will play again for ~~Belladonna~~ Bella Broomstick and ~~the big boy who looks like a troll~~ her partner.

## The tune I will play is called Magpie Number 1.

"Magpie?" I gasped. I hadn't seen the creepy bird since before the knockouts, but I knew for sure now that it had been Aunt Hemlock spying on me for all these weeks.

But why? That's what I wanted to know. Since her spell failed on Merrymeet Hill, she knew she couldn't use magic to take me back and force me to be her servant in the Magic Realm. So why was she still here? And why had she helped me to reach the Grand Final?

Whatever the reason, I felt more and more certain that she was up to something bad. I didn't like it one little bit.

But Knox was really excited by the note.

"This is great," he cried. "You saw how

much better we danced when the old lady was playing the music live. It was like I could feel the rhythm in my feet!"

I still had no idea how to tell him we would never have reached the Grand Final at all if that little old lady – who was really the meanest witch in the Magic Realm – hadn't used magic to cheat.

Mrs Spinner smiled. "If you think having the piano for the performance helps you, Knox, that sounds like a good idea," she said. "But I should warn you, I had a look this morning and managed to find a funny old recording of *Magpie Number 1* online..." She went over to the computer and turned the music on. "It's a quickstep. As the name suggests, that means you'll have to dance really fast!"

She was right! I felt breathless just listening to the music.

Dancing to it was almost impossible. Without Aunt Hemlock's magic playing to help us in rehearsals, Knox and I were just as hopeless as we had ever been. Worse! The frantic quickstep was so much trickier than the simple waltz we had done before.

"Never mind. Some performers are like that," said Mrs Spinner kindly. "They don't do very well in practice and then in performance they suddenly shine."

But, as the week slipped by, she sounded less and less sure. The new dance meant that Knox wasn't just treading on my toes; he kept tripping me up as well.

"Whoops! Sorry! ... Whoops! Sorry! ... Whoops! I'm *so* sorry, Bella," he kept saying.

"It's not your fault," I told

him. And it wasn't. He had been pushed too far. The dance was much too difficult for either of us.

The twins, meanwhile, were brilliant. While their Charleston in the first round had been snappy and fun, their tango was magnificent – all simmering and serious, like something you'd see professional grown-ups do on the real *Strictly Sequins*. Just watching them gave me bats in my belly, it was so exciting.

When they weren't practising in the village hall, they were tangoing down the corridors at school, or round the climbing frame at break.

Knox and I rehearsed in the playground every day again too – even though people had started to gather round and giggle about how hopeless we were. We needed all the practice we could get.

Of all the finalists, only Esme and Piers were keeping their new dance routine secret.

"You can't be too careful, with spies and liars and cheats around," said Piers, shooting me a nasty look.

Esme still wasn't speaking to me at all. She did watch us practising sometimes, leaning against the playground railings with her arms folded and one eyebrow raised, as we tried to learn the steps. But even all that extra effort didn't help much. I think we were getting worse, not better.

By the end of an extra-long rehearsal with Mrs Spinner on Friday night, Knox was close to tears.

"See you in the morning for our last practice ever," he said miserably as we left the village hall. "Then it's the real thing, Bella. Tomorrow night!"

He looked so worried that I almost hoped Aunt Hemlock would turn up again and play her magic music at the Grand Final. Almost – but not quite.

"Oh, Rascal, I don't know what to do," I said, stroking the little grey kitten as I tried to get to sleep that night. "If only I had my wand back by now!" If I did, I'd try to fight against Aunt Hemlock's magic – even if it meant Knox would be disappointed and we'd both look like fools if we had to perform without her help.

At least, that way, it would be a fair contest between Esme and Piers and the twins. One of them would win the trophy.

But it was hopeless. I had promised to give up my wand for a whole month. And January wasn't finished yet. The Grand Final was tomorrow evening – on the

31st – the very last night of the month. I wouldn't get my wand back until the morning after.

Whatever happened at the Grand Final tomorrow night, it would be over hours before I could use my own magic again.

# Chapter Sixteen

On the morning of the Grand Final, Uncle Martin got up early to go birdwatching on the marshes.

I was already awake. In fact, I was so worried about the performance, I had barely slept a wink all night – and whenever I did manage to drop off, I had horrible dreams about magpies dancing the quickstep. Aunty Rose was up too, hard at work with her needle and thread making my costume.

She'd shut herself away in her bedroom and wouldn't show me till it was done – but she assured me it was going to be really special.

"I'll leave you to it. There's a rare sort of warbler I want to spot," Uncle Martin explained, stuffing a thermos of coffee and some sandwiches into his rucksack.

Really, I think he was trying to keep out of the way so Aunty Rose didn't ask him to help sew on any more sequins.

"Don't worry, I'll definitely be back by six o'clock in time for the show this evening," he said as my tummy flipped over with nerves. I still couldn't quite believe that the Grand Final was only a few hours away.

"I wouldn't miss it for the world!" Uncle Martin beamed. "Our little Bella, swooping round the dance floor – I can't wait." He ruffled my curls and hurried out.

"Good luck with the warbler!" I

swallowed. Somehow seeing him so proud of me made everything a thousand times worse.

An hour later, I was still pushing a slice of toast around my plate – too nervous to eat anything – when Aunty Rose came downstairs with a tape measure around her neck and pins stuck in her cuff.

"Come on," she said, "gobble up that toast. I'll take a break and walk you down to the village for your last rehearsal."

"Thanks," I said, but the toast tasted like cardboard in my mouth and I must have sounded worried because Aunty Rose looked at me over the top of the little round glasses she always wears for sewing.

"Oh, Bella, pet – are you nervous?" she asked.

I nodded and she drew me in to a big cosy hug. "You really don't need to be," she said. "You danced so brilliantly in the knockouts and, whatever happens in the final, Uncle Martin and I will still be so proud of you."

"I know," I said, swallowing the last of the toast before it stuck in my throat. Suddenly I wished more than anything that I was going out there as ordinary Bella Broomstick, with Knox treading all over my toes ... just having fun and doing the very best we could.

"Ready?" said Aunty Rose, glancing at the clock. "We better not keep Mrs Spinner waiting."

"Ready!" I sighed, grabbing my coat and following her out of the front door.

As we stepped out on to the garden path, I wished I could tell her I didn't want to take part in the final at all. But she'd already done so much work, secretly sewing our surprise costumes from dawn till dusk. And Knox had put in all those hours of practice too – and Mrs Spinner, helping us with the routine, just as much as she had helped her own twins. It was no good. Like a cork popping out of a bottle, I was heading for that final. Nothing could stop that now.

"Look, Bella!" cried Aunty Rose, pointing to the path. "That must be a lucky sign."

There, right in front of our feet, was a single black-and-white feather.

"It's from a magpie – like the tune to your dance! You could wear it in your hair tonight," said Aunty Rose excitedly. "It would look good with the costume I've designed." She bent to pick the feather up.

"Put it down!" I almost screamed. "I don't want it. Please!"

"All right!" Aunty Rose looked surprised. "It doesn't matter." For a minute, I thought she was going to drop it. But she changed her mind. "*I'll* wear it instead," she said. "It will bring you good luck from the audience."

And she stuck the feather into the back of her hair.

"There!" She smiled and took my arm. "Come on, or we really will be late for your last rehearsal."

But when we reached the hall, instead of taking me inside where Mrs Spinner was waiting, Aunty Rose pressed her nose against the window outside the front of the building and stared through the glass.

"Aunty Rose? What are you doing?" I asked. She reminded me of something . . . and then I remembered Esme last week, when we passed Merrymeet Sweet Shop and how she'd stared in at all the jars of sweets she longed to eat.

But it wasn't sweets Aunty Rose was staring at it. It was the Glitter-Ball Trophy.

"Isn't it pretty, Bella?" she said. "So sparkly..."

"Yes," I agreed. It *was* pretty. The morning sun was shining on the window and the trophy glinted like real diamonds.

"I want it!" said Aunty Rose.

"Pardon?" I was sure I hadn't heard her right. But Aunty Rose was behaving very strangely...

"I want that pretty trophy," she said, gripping my shoulder. "I want you to win it for me, Bella."

Her big round eyes, which were normally as bright and twinkly as sapphires, were narrow and as cold as ice.

"Win it," she hissed. "Win it for me at the Grand Final tonight."

"A-Aunty Rose?" What was happening to her? She had never spoken to me like that ever before. When we'd left home just now, she'd reminded me that the competition was only a bit of fun. Now she sounded like Malinda's dad – Mr Victor – or worse. She sounded like Aunt Hemlock used to back in the Magic Realm.

She was staring through the window, hoping from foot to foot like an excited bird ... like a magpie ... desperate to reach the shiny treasure on the other side of the glass.

"A magpie!" I whispered. "Of course! The feather!" Aunty Rose had changed the minute she picked it up from the path. Now she was acting like a magpie herself. As if nothing mattered but the glittering trophy.

The feather must be cursed or enchanted in some way. "Aunt Hemlock!" I gasped.

She must have left it on the path for us to find. But – why? What did she have to gain by enchanting my lovely Aunty Rose?

I stretched out my hand and tried to pull the feather out of the back of Aunty Rose's hair. At first I tugged gently, but it wouldn't shift. I pulled harder. Aunty Rose didn't seem to feel a thing. She just stared in the window, transfixed.

"Look!" She was almost squawking with excitement. "Look how pretty the glitter ball is. Look how it sparkles."

The feather wouldn't move. It was as if it was glued to her head ... or had taken root there.

"Aunty Rose, come away," I said gently. "I've got to go. It's time for my rehearsal."

I didn't like to leave her like this. I

didn't know what to do. If I'd had my wand, perhaps I could have tried to undo the magpie curse for myself. But I had nothing...

She turned from the window at last. Her deep blue eyes looked silvery-grey.

"Yes, hurry! Go to your rehearsal." She tried to shoo me away. "You must practise your steps until you are perfect. Absolutely perfect. Do you hear me? No mistakes at all."

"I – I don't know if that's possible," I said. "Knox and I – well, we try our best, but..."

"I don't want to hear excuses. You must just try harder! Kick higher! Spin faster!" She gripped my shoulder – hard. "I want that glitter ball, Bella Broomstick," she said. "If you do not win that trophy at the Grand Final, then do not bother coming home tonight. If you do not win it for me, I – I will disown you!"

"Disown me? Aunty Rose?" I couldn't believe what I was hearing. "You – you mean...?" I couldn't even say the words. My heart was pounding like a hammer in cauldron factory and my throat was as tight as a spring. "You mean ... if I don't win the trophy, you won't want to foster me any more?"

"That's exactly what I mean," said Aunty Rose. She pressed her hand against the cold glass of the window. "If you don't win that trophy, I will not want you as my child," she said.

# Chapter Seventeen

My dancing in the rehearsal was the worst it had ever been. My stomach felt so tight, I could barely move for worrying about what had happened to Aunty Rose.

When I got home, she was polishing the mantelpiece above the fire. She had moved all the family photos and put them in a drawer — even the silver-framed one of me and her and Uncle Martin the day they fostered me. And my first day at

Merrymeet Primary. And the new one of all of us with Rascal in front of the Christmas tree.

"But I love those photos," I said.

"Never mind about photographs. This is where I am going to put the trophy when you win it," she said, polishing the wood with her cloth. It was as if she had packed away our whole life together and put it out of sight. All the love we had shared was shoved in a dusty drawer. All for a silly shiny trophy.

"Oh, Aunty Rose." I held out my hand towards her, but she turned away and carried on polishing.

"Oughtn't you be practising, Bella?" she said. "Go upstairs and run through your moves in front of the mirror."

I hesitated. This wasn't my lovely, kind, gentle Aunty Rose. How long would she stay under this horrible curse? Wasn't there anything I could do to break it?

My head was spinning like a spider on a web.

How did all this fit into Aunt Hemlock's mysterious plans?

If only Uncle Martin would come home. But he was still out on the marshes, birdwatching somewhere. He wouldn't be home for hours. And even if he did come back – which he wouldn't – how could I explain what was happening? He didn't even know I was a witch.

Suddenly, more than ever, I wanted to speak to Esme. She was the only person who would understand. She might even have one of her brilliant ideas... Yes! I was sure she'd be able to help – if only I could get her to listen. "Aunty Rose? Can I use the phone?" I said.

"Hmm?" She barely looked up as I ran to the kitchen. I was going to call Esme at the windmill. If I could just get her to believe that it really was Aunt Hemlock who had used magic to get me through to the final, then I could explain everything. I could tell her that Aunty Rose was under a terrible curse.

But when Mrs Lee answered the phone, she said that Esme wasn't in. "I'm sorry, Bella. She went off with Piers, first thing," she explained. "They're going to be at the fancy dance studio all day. Mrs Seymour has paid for a whole block of extra lessons – something about a tricky move they need to practise... They'll only be back in Merrymeet in time for the competition tonight."

"Oh!" My heart sank. "Maybe I could try her mobile," I said desperately. I knew her mum had given her one for emergencies. And this was an emergency ... for me! And for Aunty Rose too.

"Sorry," said Mrs Lee. "It's sitting right here on the kitchen table. You know how forgetful Esme is. Apparently they're really strict about phones at the dance studio anyway."

"I see... Thank you," I said – wishing that I could leap on a broomstick and fly to the studio myself.

"Good luck tonight, Bella!" said Mrs Lee brightly as we hung up.

*I'm going to need it*, I thought, glancing out of the window. Sure enough, I saw that the Seymours' car was gone from the drive next door. If Esme's mum was right, Piers would be at the dance studio all day too.

Piers and Esme were the only Persons in the whole of Merrymeet who knew I was a witch. They were the only ones who wouldn't think I was as mad as a werewolf at a full moon if I tried to explain that I thought Aunty Rose might have fallen under some kind of terrible enchantment. But I couldn't get hold of either of them ... and even if I could, they weren't talking to me anyway.

I went upstairs and cried helplessly into Rascal's fur, until Aunty Rose banged on the door and told me it was time to get dressed.

As she laid my costume on the bed, I gasped.

She had made me a floaty black-and-white dress with a long feathery fringe around the hem – it was all covered in hundreds of shiny black-and-white sequins.

"A magpie dress for your magpie tune!" said Aunty Rose proudly.

But I felt as if a giant was kneeling on my chest. I could barely breathe.

"Hurry up! Put in on!" Aunty Rose clapped her hands and helped me get dressed.

I was still in a daze as she ushered me out of the bedroom. There was something truly horrible about being dressed up as the bird I had come to fear so much.

But Aunty Rose kept pushing me forward, poking me in the small of my back.

We were halfway down the stairs when Uncle Martin came through the front door with his binoculars round his neck.

"Oh, Uncle Martin! I'm so pleased to see you," I cried.

He looked up at me, and smiled.

"What a perfect costume! I hope it will

make you win the trophy, Bella," he said. "We want that trophy, you know,"

The moment I heard the coldness in his voice, I knew that he was bewitched too.

"No. . .!" There was so much I wanted to say, but I didn't know where to start. "Did you spot the warbler?" I asked, longing to catch a glimmer of the old excitement he would usually show when he returned from a birdwatching trip.

"Better than that. I saw a wonderful magpie," he said. But although his eyes were glistening, they seemed grey and cold.

"A magpie?" I should have known. "But aren't magpies common, ordinary birds?" I asked. "You told me once they were horrible thieves. Taking eggs from other birds' nests."

"Not this one. This one was special," said

Uncle Martin. "It dropped a feather on the ground right beside me. It let it fall from its beak, as if it was giving me a gift."

I shuddered as he pointed to a scraggy black-and-white feather stuck in the rim of his hat.

Aunty Rose squealed with delight. She had already changed into her best black frock with neat white tights. But she was still wearing her magpie feather in her hair.

"Hurry up now, Martin. It's nearly time to leave. You better go and change," she said, bustling him upstairs. "We don't want to make Bella late. This is a *very* important night for her."

"Yes!" he said, glaring into my eyes as he passed me on the bottom step. "We expect great things this evening. We expect you to bring that trophy home to us, Bella."

When he came downstairs a few minutes later, he was looking smarter than I had ever seen him. He was wearing a black suit with shiny ebony shoes and a crisp white shirt. The magpie feather was poking out of his jacket pocket like a handkerchief.

"Ready?" he asked. And without waiting for an answer they both bundled me out of the front door and into the car.

All the way to the village hall, they kept talking about how important it was for me to win the trophy. How it was the only thing they cared about...

I tried to block out what they were saying. After all, it wasn't really them who were speaking. It was all a horrible curse. I tried to breathe deeply. But my legs were wobbling and my tummy was swirling faster than a dancer in the Viennese waltz.

"Look!" Uncle Martin skidded to a stop outside the village hall.

"What's wrong?" I asked.

But Aunty Rose was already scrambling out of the car.

"It's gone!" she cried, pointing to the empty window where the trophy had been. Uncle Martin pushed past and they dashed ahead of me into the hall.

I followed, pulling my big red coat tightly around me to hide my costume underneath.

The hall was buzzing with people, all pushing to the front trying to get a look at the judges, who were already sitting behind their table at the edge of the stage.

Miss Swan was wearing a bright pink dress and her silvery hair was in a tight bun on top of her head – just like a proper ballet

dancer. Lady Trim had a purple ball gown and huge sparkly earrings which looked like real diamonds. Wane sat between them, wearing a green sequin suit. He was licking his lips and glancing nervously around the hall.

Was he looking for Aunt Hemlock? Was she here already? I searched the crowd but there was no sign of her – not even in her little old lady disguise.

I could see Uncle Martin and Aunty Rose though. They had already pushed themselves right to the front of the crowd.

The Glitter-Ball Trophy had pride of place, shimmering in the middle of the judges' table. Uncle Martin and Aunty Rose were stretching out their hands trying to touch it.

"Oi! Move out the way, will you. I want to get a picture," roared a photographer. There were at least five or six of them this time. Not just the skinny man from the *Merrymeet Mercury*. They were all clicking their cameras as their flashes went off like fireworks.

"Excuse me? Mr Smyles? Over here!" roared a woman with a microphone. I saw her push Aunty Rose out of the way. "This is for the local radio. Can you tell us how you feel to be judging the Grand Final here tonight?"

Wane looked baffled for a moment, as if he had no idea what he was supposed to say. Then he grabbed the glittering trophy in his leathery hands and held it high above his head.

"Gladies and lentlemen, I mean ladies and gentlemen," he cried. "This is what tonight is all about! There is only one thing that matters and that is winning this glitter-ball prize."

"I thought it was about having fun!" said a voice behind me.

I spun around and saw Zac. He was standing on tiptoe, trying to get a look at the judges too.

Zoe was beckoning to us both from the dressing door.

"I suppose we'd better go," sighed Zac, who was wearing a coat buttoned over his costume too. "Otherwise we'll be in trouble for being out front before the show."

"I suppose so," I agreed. And I turned to

follow him. But someone grabbed my arm.

"Wait!" It was Aunty Rose. She leant forward. For a moment I thought she was going to kiss me on the cheek and wish me good luck. But instead her fingers closed like claws on my shoulder and she hissed in my ear. "Win it, Bella. Win that glitter ball. Or else. I meant what I said – without that trophy, you'll be no child of mine."

Then she followed Uncle Martin to the front row, where he was already standing guard over two seats.

I wanted to run after them. To beg them to give up their hopes of the trophy. Surely it didn't mean that much? I wanted to remind them that just a few days ago, they really had believed that this was all a bit of fun.

But Zac was already heading backstage

and I could see Mrs Spinner beckoning to me from the door.

I hurried over, desperate to see if Esme had arrived. Perhaps I could get a chance to talk to her before the show.

But the minute I came backstage, she turned her back on me. And Piers started whispering in her ear. They were both dressed in red and gold. Piers looked like a Roman solider and Esme had a little cropped top and a beautiful long skirt with ruffles like a flamenco dancer.

"You look amazing!" I gasped.

Esme nodded. "So do you," she said as I slipped out of my coat. But she still didn't smile and Piers ignored me completely.

"Wow!" Zoe touched the feathery hem on the bottom of my dress. "It's like a real bird. That's amazing."

"And your outfits are wonderful too," I

said as the twins took off their coats. They had brilliant matching flame-coloured suits which looked like orange fire.

"Thanks!" Zoe grinned as Mrs Spinner clapped her hands.

"Right, everybody. We'll keep to the same dancing order as last time," she said. "So that's Piers and Esme first. Then Zac and Zoe. Finally Bella and Knox."

I hadn't even noticed poor Knox. He was crouched in the corner like a crab. I hadn't seen his costume yet either – but as he staggered to his feet, I saw that Aunty Rose had made him a black-and-white-shiny sequin suit to match my magpie dress.

"Are you all right?" asked Mrs Spinner. Knox nodded.

"Good. In that case, do you mind if I go out to the front to watch the show today?" said Mrs Spinner. "I'm sure as there are so few of you, you can manage to be quiet and sensible backstage."

"We will!" we all promised. But as soon as she slipped out through the curtain, Knox sank to the floor again.

"I don't feel too good," he said, clutching his tummy. He was as green as a goblin and shaking with nerves.

By the time the twins and I had managed to get him to his feet, Esme and Piers were already on stage about to begin. A hush fell over the audience. I peeped out of the gap in the curtains. All the other children from Indigo Class were sitting together in the balcony to watch the show tonight. Aunty Rose and Uncle Martin were right in the middle of the front row. Mr and Mrs Seymour were beside them, along with Knox's tall smiley parents and Esme's mum with Gretel, then Mrs Spinner on the end.

The twins' dad was still helping with the music at the sound desk. Everyone in the audience was staring up at Piers and Esme as they stood ready to begin their dance. Only Aunty Rose and Uncle Martin weren't looking at them. Their eyes were turned towards the judges' table. They were staring at the glittering trophy.

I saw a movement at the back of the hall, and the door creaked shut as the figure of a little old woman in a black cloak slipped into the back row.

So Aunt Hemlock was here. She had come.

Whatever happened next, I was in her power.

# Chapter Eighteen

Esme and Piers did a brilliant paso doble.

There was a wonderful sequence in the middle where Piers stretched out his arm, still holding Esme's hand, and she spun towards him with three perfect full turns. If that was the tricky move they had spent all day practising, it was worth it. They were magnificent... Right up until the very end, when Esme seemed to miss a beat and turn her head the wrong way. It was as if she was looking at something – or someone – in the audience. She had to shuffle to try and catch up. But she was out of time with Piers by then and still seemed a little distracted.

Even so, they were amazing. The audience leapt to their feet and gave them a standing ovation at the end.

Lady Trim raised her card: 8

Miss Swan: 8

Wane licked his lips and gave his best Ken Smyles grin: 10.

The crowd cheered. It seemed to them that the famous TV star was being generous at last. Yet I wondered why Aunt Hemlock's horrible chameleon was being so kind all of a sudden. This was his first ten in the whole competition.

Piers scowled furiously at Esme as he bowed. He obviously thought they could have got a higher score from the other judges too if Esme hadn't lost her concentration at the end.

As he went to storm up to the balcony, Esme grabbed his sleeve and pulled him through the curtain backstage. "This way!" she hissed. "I need to talk to Bella."

She was frowning even more deeply than Piers. My heart sank. I had been desperate to talk to my best friend for days. But she looked so fierce, I was sure she was going to really lose her temper. Did she think it was my fault her dance had gone wrong?

"Esme, listen," I begged, but she put her finger to her lips and pointed to the twins.

"GOOD LUCK!" we all mouthed as they stepped out on to the stage.

Then Esme pushed Piers towards poor terrified Knox, who was sitting with his head between his knees against the back wall. "Go and cheer him up. Make him feel brave. He's got to go onstage in a minute," she said, giving Piers a shove. "And take this." She handed him a bucket. "Just in case. He looks like he might be sick." My heart was pounding as Esme cleared them all out of the way. I was sure she was going to tell me she didn't want to be my best friend any more.

She grabbed my hand and dragged me to the opposite corner before Piers could protest.

"Esme," I whispered. "I can explain everything..."

"Shh!" she hissed. "Not a word!" Then she pulled me towards her in a hug. "I'm so sorry, Bella. You don't need to say another thing. I should have believed you all along. I should have known you wouldn't use magic to win against your friends."

"Glorious Griffins!" A flood of relief washed over me. She wasn't angry with me after all. "What changed your mind?" My heart stopped pounding at last. No matter what else happened tonight, at least my best friend believed I was not a cheat. "Did you see Aunt Hemlock in the audience?" I asked. "Did you recognize her disguise?" Maybe that's what had made Esme lose her concentration at the end of her dance.

"No!" Esme led me to the gap in the curtain. "I saw your Aunty Rose and Uncle Martin," she whispered, pointing to the front row. Every pair of eyes in the audience was turned towards the twins. Zac was lifting Zoe as she kicked her legs in the air like scissors. It was a move they had practised time and time again in rehearsal and they had it perfect today. There was round of wild, spontaneous applause.

Only Aunty Rose and Uncle Martin weren't watching. They were staring at the trophy all the time.

"They were like that while I was dancing too," said Esme. "That's when I knew that there was something wrong. They're always so kind and encouraging. Last time I danced, your Aunty Rose smiled at me all the way through. And your Uncle Martin was the first one on his feet cheering at the end. Now they didn't even clap. They can barely take their eyes off that glittery trophy. I know something's wrong, Bella. They must be under some sort of curse."

"Exactly!" I whispered. "They're bewitched! Look at the magpie feather in Aunty Rose's hair and the one poking out of Uncle Martin's top pocket." I told Esme how finding the feather had changed Aunty Rose almost the moment she set eyes on it and how she said she would disown me if I didn't win the Glitter-Ball Trophy tonight. "Then Uncle Martin came home from birdwatching and he had one too. They were both so horrible and strict and scary."

"Oh, Bella!" Esme squeezed my hand. "Just remember, it is only some sort of evil spell that's made them like that. They adore you just as much as they would if you were their own child. They could never stop loving you, especially not because of some silly shiny prize."

I knew what she was saying was true. But it didn't help. Not really. Because, for now, my wonderful, kind foster parents were no longer themselves. They would do anything to get their hands on that glitter ball – like magpies stealing treasure for their nest.

"If only I hadn't been so stupid," said Esme. "If only I hadn't been ignoring you all week we could have tried to work this out together..."

"You couldn't have known – I can see how it must have looked," I said, peering through the curtain. "I just wish I knew what Aunt Hemlock was planning to do – and there's no time to find out..." The twins were moving towards their finale already.

"Quick, then," said Esme, "Let's think what we *do* know!"

"The only thing I'm certain of is that Aunt Hemlock is behind all this," I said.

"Right!" agreed Esme. "And we know that Aunt Hemlock wants you back. She wants you to work for her in the Magic Realm and wash her silly pots and pans. But she can't get you back because she gave you away. Unless..."

"Unless Aunty Rose and Uncle Martin don't want me any more!" I said, sinking to my knees and putting my head between my hands like poor Knox. "And if I don't win that trophy, then they won't want me! They said so themselves. Aunt Hemlock will be free to take me away," I said. "The bond of magic which has held me here will be broken."

Esme nodded. "I think that's what all this is about. Aunt Hemlock is trying to trick Martin and Rose into swapping you for the trophy."

"Of course!" I groaned. "That's why she used magic to help me in the first round. She wanted it to seem as if I had a real chance of winning."

"Just like my New Year's resolution," said Esme thoughtfully. "It would have been easy for me to give up sweets if I had never tasted them. But because I know how delicious they are, it's all I can ever think about. Now your Aunty Rose and Uncle Martin believe you can win that trophy, it's all they dream of... Especially since Aunt Hemlock put them under the magpie curse."

"Oh, Esme!" I gasped. She had put it so perfectly. But there was something else too. The second part of Aunt Hemlock's terrible plan. "She's not going to use magic to help me win tonight, is she?"

"No." Esme shook her head. "I don't think so."

"What can I do?" I said. "I've still got to go out there and dance. It's the only way I'll have any chance at all of winning that glitter ball. And if I don't win it, I'll lose Aunty Rose and Uncle Martin for ever." I swallowed down a sob. "They said they'd disown me if I didn't win the trophy. If they do that, Aunt Hemlock has won. She can take me back to the Magic Realm with her."

"If only you had your wand," said Esme. "Then you could try some magic of your own."

"I know," I said. "But there's nothing I can do. I won't get it back until tomorrow and all this will be over by then."

"Oh, Bella, I'm so sorry," Esme whispered. "These stupid New Year's resolutions were all my idea."

"Nonsense," I said. But before I could convince her it wasn't her fault, the sound of wild cheers and clapping filled the hall.

The twins' dance was finished already. The judges were holding up their cards.

"Nine!" called Lady Trim.

"Nine!" said Miss Swan.

"Ten!" wheezed Wane again.

"Well, that's blown it!" hissed Piers, who was down the other end of the long curtain, peeping out on to the stage from there. "They've beaten us now, Esme!"

"Oh, do be quiet!" she snapped. "We've got far more important things to worry about than that."

"Like what?" asked Piers.

"Like me!" said Knox, staggering to his feet. His face was a green as a frog. "I'm sorry, Bella. I just can't do it. I'm too nervous. I can't go onstage and dance!"

He sank back down to the floor and stuck his head in the bucket.

# Chapter Nineteen

Esme and Piers tried to pull Knox to his feet, but he wouldn't move.

The twins had already left the stage and gone up to the balcony. The crowd were growing restless.

"Please, Knox," I begged. "We've got to win that trophy. We've got to at least try."

I peeped out of the curtains and saw Aunt Hemlock shuffling up the aisle in her little old lady disguise. Even under her hood I could see she was grinning with delight.

"Come out," she called. "We're waiting for you, my dears."

Knox stuck his head in the bucket again. "I can't. I'm sorry."

Esme put her hand on my shoulder.

"Aunt Hemlock won't give up," I said desperately. "I have to get out there and dance, otherwise there's no chance of winning that trophy at all." And if I didn't win the glitter ball, the horrible magpie curse would make Uncle Martin and Aunty Rose think they didn't want me any more. Aunt Hemlock would be free to snatch me away. By midnight tonight, I'd be back in the Magic Realm, scrubbing cauldrons for the rest of my life. I'd never see my wonderful foster family or my friends in Merrymeet ever again.

"It's simple. Somebody else will have to dance with you if Knox can't," said Esme. "You'll need a new partner."

"Don't look at me," said Piers, leaping backwards. We hadn't had time to explain anything to him. He was probably still furious, thinking I'd used magic to cheat in the first round.

"Oh, for goodness' sake!" Esme sighed. "Knox, give me your jacket. It doesn't say anywhere in the rules that the partners have to be a boy and a girl. *I'll* dance with you, Bella," she said.

"Is everything all right?" whispered Mr Spinner, poking his head through the curtains. "Only your pianist seems to be getting a bit impatient, Bella."

Aunt Hemlock was banging the lid of the piano up and down, like a door in the wind.

"Hurry up, my dears!" she cackled.

"Ready?" said Mr Spinner encouragingly. Then his eyes fell on Knox. "Oh dear!"

"Don't worry!" said Esme. "There's been a tiny change of plan, that's all. Perhaps you could announce that Bella has a new dance partner ... me!"

She had pulled Knox's huge black-and-white jacket over her little cropped top and slipped out of her flamenco skirt. The jacket was so long on her that it was like a dress.

"Perfect!" she said, taking Knox's tie too and knotting it around her waist like a sash as we heard Mr Spinner making his announcement onstage.

"In a last-minute change of contestants, Bella Broomstick will dance with Esme Lee."

"But you don't know the moves," I

whispered as she pulled me towards the curtain.

"Yes, I do," said Esme. "Some of them, at least. I've seen you practising in the playground."

"Some of them? But what about the moves you don't know?" I asked.

"For those," said Esme calmly, "we'll just have to make something up!"

Esme and I stood side by side in the middle of the stage.

The audience fell silent and I heard Aunt Hemlock crack her knuckles behind us. Then she tinkled on the piano keys.

"Ready, my dears?" she said, and the tune to *Magpie Number 1* began to play.

The moment the music started, I slid my foot across the floor, and I knew for certain that no magic was going to help us this time.

There was no tingle or lift, no floating feeling. Just me and my ordinary dancing — more like a flat-footed bear than a ballroom star.

I swung left at exactly the same moment Esme swung right.

BAM!

We almost knocked each other to the floor.

I stumbled for a moment, almost falling on top of Aunt Hemlock at the piano. The crowd gasped. She looked over her shoulder and grinned at me — not a friendly smile this time, but the mean sneer I knew so well.

"Clumsy as ever, I see! Oh yes — you're coming home with me, Belladonna Broomstick!" she cackled, just loud enough so that I could hear her on the stage but, under the sound of swelling music, the audience wouldn't hear a thing. "You're not going to win that trophy now, are you? And if you *don't* win, your sweet little aunty and uncle won't want you any more. Such a pity!"

I tried desperately to block her out of my mind. I tried to get back to the quickstep routine. Aunt Hemlock was right; of course the trophy was probably lost already – our first few moves had been a disaster. But I had to try – I had to try my very best to win that glitter ball.

"This way," I mouthed, shimmying to the left, hoping Esme would be able to remember enough of the routine.

She smiled and followed my lead with a flourish. It wasn't bad, but there was no way this was a trophy-winning performance. Especially not after the twins' spectacular tango and Piers and Esme's nearly perfect paso doble.

I wanted to sit down on the floor and cry. I wanted to give up. But I couldn't. I was standing onstage with the whole of Merrymeet watching me. I had to give them some sort of show.

I could already hear some of the audience giggling. I don't think they were sure if it was meant to be a funny routine or not.

I lifted my head, threw my shoulders back and did a quarter turn. But things got worse. As I stepped away, Esme's foot caught on the hem of my feathery dress and there was a ripping sound. A patter of sequins scattered across the floor.

Out of the corner of my eye, I saw Aunty Rose glance in our direction. At last she had taken her eyes off the trophy for a moment. I raised my arm and tried to spin off on a diagonal, but Esme was still standing on the ragged hem of my dress. I tugged at it with one hand while waving the other in the air and trying to make it look as if it was all part of a complicated move. But it was no good. My hem was caught around Esme's heel. The audience laughed – a nervous wave of giggles.

Every time Esme moved, the threads of my dress were pulled and another little shower of sequins fell to the floor.

I saw Aunty Rose leaning forward in the front row, peering at the floor of the stage.

It was the shimmer of the fallen sequins she was looking at. Uncle Martin had spotted them too. He was stretching out his hand as if he wanted to touch them. I gasped. The shiny sequins had made them forget about the trophy for a moment. They both stared at the little glittery treasures, bobbing their heads, with tiny bird-like movements ... like a pair of magpies.

Esme grabbed me by the hand and spun me round as more sequins scattered from the frayed end of my dress. We had given up all pretence of trying to do the quickstep by now. In fact, I was pretty much just waving my arms and swaying while Esme leapt around me.

Esme might not have been following a routine, but she was dancing brilliantly. A bold, funny dance, that made the audience laugh out loud instead of the nervous giggles of a moment earlier. She was sliding and twirling and swirling and leaping so high it looked as if she might touch the glittering stars on the ceiling.

That's what gave me the idea...

"Leap as high as you can, Esme!" I begged as she swirled past me again. "Leap so high, you can grab a star."

I had seen the way Aunty Rose and Uncle Martin looked at the falling sequins. But such tiny sparkles weren't going to keep their attention for long. Not with the glittering trophy still shining like a lighthouse on the judges' table.

I needed Aunty Rose and Uncle Martin to forget about that trophy. I needed them to look at me instead. If I could just get their attention, then maybe the curse could be broken. Maybe I could remind them both that they loved me – that they didn't mind if I got one out of ten in a spelling test or if I didn't bring a shiny trophy home – just so long as I tried my best.

I had a plan at last... But to make it work, we needed to gather as many glittering, sparkling, shiny things in front of Aunty Rose and Uncle Martin as we could.

And all before the end of the song.

# Chapter Twenty

Aunt Hemlock kept turning round on her piano stool and sneering at me. She was only pretending to play, of course, while magic did all the work.

"Quick, Esme," I whispered again, "grab a hanging star if you can." Aunty Rose and Uncle Martin were like magpies, drawn to anything shiny. "We need to get their attention away from that trophy ... and fast." I knew we didn't have long. The song was almost over. By the time it was finished, we would have to leave the stage and our last chance would be gone.

I tried to leap for a star too. Esme was like a ballet dancer – I was more like a frog. I knew I wasn't going to jump high enough to reach one. Instead I spun towards the piano – right under Aunt Hemlock's nose. I snatched a string of tinsel and spun away again.

"Oh dear," I heard Miss Swan say at the judges' table, "this really isn't a quickstep. I don't actually know what it is. I'm not going to be able to give them any points at all."

"Disqualify them," roared Wane.

I didn't mind about that. I knew there was no chance we would win the competition. Not any more. Aunty Rose and Uncle Martin would never get their shimmering trophy. But I wanted to give them something far better. If my plan worked, I was hoping I could give them back our love. I wouldn't let Aunt Hemlock ruin that. And I wouldn't let her take me back to the Magic Realm either... Just so long as Esme and I could grab every shiny thing we could see before the music stopped.

Esme was holding a star over her head. I draped the string of tinsel round my shoulders and stretched out my hands towards her.

"What exactly are we doing?" she whispered, never missing a step of the tap dance she had broken into as she handed me the glittering star.

"Magic!" I said. I might not have a wand, but I didn't need it! "This is homemade magic." I grinned.

Esme's eyes widened, but without asking

any more questions, she reached for another star and a silver streamer too.

Aunty Rose's eyes darted over towards the shining trophy. Uncle Martin followed her gaze. I had to get their attention back again.

I slid across the floor and took a long, pearly ribbon from the curtain, sending sequins scattering like enchanted raindrops.

Esme spun me round, winding the streamer round me like a maypole.

Soon, I could barely move or dance at all. I had more tinsel and streamers wound around me than the brightest Christmas tree.

Mr Richards, the guitar teacher, who was up in the lighting box, shone a spotlight on me and I sparkled.

Then the last notes of *Magpie Number 1* faded and the song was done.

The audience clapped – a little unsure at first. I am sure they were totally confused by what they had seen. But Esme took such a big, bold bow and gestured towards me with such flourish that they soon clapped louder, and some of them even cheered.

I kept my eyes on Aunty Rose and Uncle Martin. They were looking in my direction – blinking as the stars and tinsel wrapped all around me shimmered.

As the audience fell quiet, I cleared my throat.

"Ladies and gentlemen ... and judges," I said. "I am sorry you did not get to see us dance a proper quickstep. I know I will be disqualified from the competition, but..." I took a deep breath and tried to stop my voice from shaking. "But before we leave the stage, I just wanted to say something, if I may."

I glanced towards the judges' table. Wane shook his head but I ignored him as Lady Trim and Miss Swan nodded. I could feel Aunt Hemlock's eyes boring into the back of my neck.

"I want to say thank you to all of you who have welcomed me to Merrymeet Village," I said. "I have not lived here long, but I feel it is my home." There was a burst of applause and I heard Aunt Hemlock hiss.

"Most of all," I said, "I want to thank my Uncle Martin and my Aunty Rose for being the best foster parents ever. I know they wanted me to win the Glitter–Ball Trophy tonight ... Aunty Rose has even cleared a space on the mantelpiece..." The audience laughed. They thought I was joking. But I knew this was the most important speech I would ever make. I needed to remind my foster parents of our love. "I cannot win the

Glitter-Ball Trophy for you, Aunty Rose and Uncle Martin," I said. "So instead ... I have made myself into a glitter ball!"

"Ta da!" Esme gestured towards me. I was standing in the middle of the stage covered from head to toe in shimmering silver. "Ladies and gentlemen," she said, "I present Bella Broomstick: The Amazing Glitter-Ball Girl!"

There was another cheer from the audience.

"I know I am not a real trophy," I said, keeping my eyes on Aunty Rose and Uncle Martin all the time. My words seemed to be getting through to them at last. They seemed to be leaning forward and listening to me. Their eyes looked warm and deep again, not blank and shiny like silver coins. "I am too big to fit on the mantelpiece," I went on. "And I can't stay wrapped up in

tinsel and sequins for ever. But…" I bit my lip. "But if you could see into my heart, you would know that it is shining brighter than any glitter ball. It is shining with so much love for you!"

"Oh, Bella!" Aunty Rose was on her feet in an instant. The next thing I knew her arms were around me. And Uncle Martin was up on the stage and hugging me too.

"Sweetheart! Forgive us!" he implored.

"I don't know what got into us," whispered Aunty Rose. "We don't want any fancy trophies or silly prizes. You are the best thing that ever happened to us."

"Thank you!" I whispered, and as they were hugging me, I slipped the magpie feather out of Uncle Martin's pocket and stretched up to take the other one from Aunty Rose's hair. The moment my fingers touched them, the feathers turned to dust – a sort of silver glitter – that shimmered for a moment and disappeared.

Aunt Hemlock's spell was destroyed for good. She could not take me away from my new family or my friends. She could not take me back to the Magic Realm. I had beaten her ... not with magic – not even with shiny sequins and tinsel – but with love. And with my best friend's help, of course!

I heard Aunt Hemlock let out a furious cackle from behind me. But by the time I turned to the piano, she was gone.

At the judges' table, Wane had vanished too.

Afterwards, nobody ever knew where the old lady who had played the piano or Ken Smyles, the famous TV dance judge, had disappeared to.

"I expect Ken Smyles had to hurry away;

celebrities are always very busy, you know," said Mrs Seymour.

"Perhaps the old lady was tired after all that frantic piano playing," said Mr Spinner.

I think it was only Esme and I who spotted a scruffy magpie flying away through the rafters and a small cross-looking lizard scuttling down the aisle.

But, by then, we were already leaving the stage ourselves. We had been in the spotlight far too long already.

It was time to cheer for the twins – the true champions of *Strictly Merrymeet*, who deserved to win the Glitter-Ball Trophy so very much.

# Chapter Twenty-One

After the show was finally over, we all stayed to tidy up.

"Although Bella and Esme have done most of the work already." Uncle Martin laughed. "They've taken down half the decorations to make their human glitter ball!"

As soon as I saw Mrs Spinner, I ran over and apologized to her for our terrible quickstep routine. "Especially after you had taken so much time to teach me and Knox the real steps."

"Don't worry," she said. "It's a pity you and Esme were disqualified. The dance you did wasn't strictly ballroom – but it was a lot of a fun!"

"And that is *all* that matters," said Aunty Rose, gathering me into another hug. And it was true!

Even poor Knox looked a little less green now.

"I'm sorry I lost my nerve and couldn't go onstage," he said.

"It doesn't matter one little bit," I told him. "You were a brilliant partner anyway." And I saw he had put his name at the very top of the list which Mrs Spinner was passing round to see if anyone would be interesting in doing regular ballroom dancing lessons (just for fun!).

"I'd like to learn more proper steps," he said. "Then who knows what I might be able to do!"

"Good for you, Knox," agreed Mrs Spinner. And Esme and I signed up too, as well as the twins of course. And most of Indigo Class.

Only Piers refused.

"I'm never dancing again," he grumbled. He was still in a foul mood even though I had told him everything and he knew that I hadn't used magic to cheat. He just likes winning, I think. But I knew Esme and I would persuade him to come to the classes in the end. Even though he'd probably insist on being very grumpy about it.

When the tidying up was nearly finished, Esme grabbed my hand and dragged me outside.

"I'm sorry I ever doubted you," she

apologized, a hot blush creeping up her cheeks. "I can't believe I said all those terrible things about you being a witch..."

I stuck my fingers in my ears and refused to listen.

"You were right to be angry," I said. "You thought I was cheating and that wouldn't have been fair. You are my very best friend and if it wasn't for you, I'd be heading back to the Magic Realm on the back of Aunt Hemlock's broomstick by now."

We both glanced up at the sky and shuddered. But there was no one there.

"Look!" I said, pointing to the bright face of the church clock. "It's nearly midnight again."

"The witching hour!" said Aunty Rose, coming out of the hall to find us.

"Nonsense!" I said, linking arms with her. "There are no witches in Merrymeet!"

"Or no wicked ones at least!" Esme muttered under her breath.

"Come on!" said Aunty Rose. "The tidying up's all done now. It's time we went home."

"I'd like that," I said. And she hurried inside to find Uncle Martin with the car keys.

Esme and I were still standing on the front steps of the hall as the clock struck midnight.

"Pinch punch for the first of the month!" she said, tweaking my nose as the gongs died away. "It's February now!"

"And I can get my beautiful wand back today," I whispered.

"And I can eat this!" Esme dug into her coat pocket and pulled out the chocolate coin I had given her on New Year's Day.

"Dancing Dervishes, we should celebrate!" I said, as Piers came out of the hall too. "I tell you what. I'll take you both to Merrymeet Sweet Shop as soon as it's open and buy you each a giant gobstopper ... if such a magical thing really *does* exist in the Person World!"

"You'll see!" said Piers, smiling at last. "But you won't be able to believe how big they are!"

I couldn't wait to try a gobstopper for myself. But, before we went to the sweet shop, there was something much more important that I needed to do. I needed to go to the top of Merrymeet Hill ... just as soon as it was light enough in the morning.

*

Esme stayed at my house for a sleepover again, and Aunty Rose made pancakes for breakfast.

"Thank goodness January is over!" Esme grinned as she smothered her third pancake with chocolate spread *and* mini marshmallow sprinkles.

"Exactly!" I agreed, doing the same. Then I asked Uncle Martin and Aunty Rose if Esme and I could go for a walk.

"Of course you can!" they said.

Once we had loaded the dishwasher (I can NEVER get over what a magical Person invention it is), I hurried to the hall and pulled on my coat. Before I stepped out of the front door, I turned and took both my foster parents by the hand.

"I love you more than anything in the whole wide world!" I said.

"And we love you too!" Uncle Martin's

voice cracked as he ruffled my hair.

"More than anything!" whispered Aunty Rose. "You are the most precious thing in our lives, Bella. And we don't need any trophy to prove that."

"Thank you!" I said. As I looked over her shoulder I saw that the family photographs were back in pride of place on the mantelpiece – exactly where they should be.

"Just one more thing," I whispered to Esme, "and everything will be perfect again." In the end I hadn't needed magic to win Aunty Rose and Uncle Martin back. Love – and a home-made sequin trophy – had been stronger than any spell.

Even so, I couldn't wait to get my beloved flamingo back. I knew I'd feel safer with a wand in my pocket ... just in case.

"I've missed your magic almost as much

as sweets and chocolate!" puffed Esme as we scrambled to the top of Merrymeet Hill. "When you get your wand back, will you do some teeny-tiny spells? . . . Just for fun!"

"You know I shouldn't!" I said firmly. But Esme was right. It would be lovely to be able to tidy my room with magic again, or give Esme rainbow stripes in her hair, or turn a bar of soap into a little fish to play with in the bath – all with the tap of a wand. Just as long as no one saw me. . .

As we reached the brow of the hill, I spread my arms wide and looked up into the sky.

*Oh, precious wand, the month*
*is done,*
*So hurry back. . .*

"Er..." I stopped dead. My mind was a blank as I tried to think how to end the rest of spell with a rhyme.

"Hold on! I've got it!" Esme nudged me and whispered something in my ear.

"Oh, all right! Why not?" I smiled and repeated what she had told me.

*Oh, precious wand, the month is done,*
*So hurry back ... for some magic fun!*

As I looked up, I saw a bright streak of pink in the grey morning sky, and my beautiful flamingo flew into view.

"Welcome home!" I whispered as she landed on the hill beside us. A shimmer of magic glitter sparkled like sequins on the grass.

Turn the page to read
the beginning of Bella's
first adventure!

I'm drawing this with a stick and swamp mud!

# Chapter One

I am a hopeless witch.

Everybody says so.

Especially Aunt Hemlock. She woke me up at dawn this morning just to tell me how hopeless I am.

"Belladonna Broomstick, you are the most hopeless young witch in the whole of the Magic Realm!" she said, poking me with her long fingernails as the seven warts on the end of her nose wobbled like fat green frogs.

I don't have any warts on my nose. Perhaps that's why I'm such a hopeless witch?

If I could grow just one teeny-tiny wart, I might learn to be good at magic.

I yawned and peeped at my reflection in Aunt Hemlock's magic mirror.

"Aha!" cackled the mirror. "If it's not

Belladonna Broomstick. Just look at your big brown eyes and chocolate curls. Not a wart in sight. Pathetic. What a hopeless young witch!"

"Actually, Bella, I think you're very pretty," whispered a spider that swung down from the roof of the cave.

"Thank you," I blushed, understanding every word he'd said. Speaking animal languages is the only thing I am any good at.

## Belladonna Broomstick's Magic Skills

Wand Work: HOPELESS
Spells: HOPELESS
Potions: HOPELESS
Talking to Animals: EXCELLENT!! *YIPPEE!*

"Quiet!" Aunt Hemlock grabbed the poor little spider by seven of his eight long legs and dunked him in her lumpy porridge.

"Let him go!" I cried.

As if by magic (which it probably was), Aunt Hemlock's creepy chameleon, Wane, appeared on the kitchen shelf. Wane gives me the shivers. I never know what colour he is going to be or where he will appear next. He's always spying on me and telling tales to Aunt Hemlock. Right now he was disguising himself behind a jar of frogspawn.

"Yum! Is that spider for me, mistress?" he slurped, sticking out his long purple tongue.

"Certainly not!" Aunt Hemlock dangled the spider above her open mouth. "This one is mine."

"Stop!" I begged, but Aunt Hemlock swallowed the poor thing whole. "How

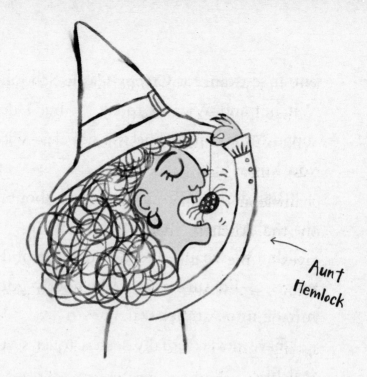

Aunt Hemlock

horrible!" I shuddered.

"And very unfair not to share," sulked Wane, turning piglet-pink in a huff.

Aunt Hemlock ignored us both and picked her teeth with a chicken bone.

"You're looking marvellously magical today, if I may say so, mistress," said the mirror, sucking up to her as usual.

"At least one of us is looking magical," sighed Aunt Hemlock. "Belladonna has her entrance exam for Creepy Castle School for Witches and Wizards today ... but I don't suppose she'll pass. She is a hopeless witch, you know."

"Belladonna Broomstick is about as magical as mud," agreed the mirror.

I know what I'd do if I was good at magic... I'd turn that vain, goody-goody mirror into a toilet seat.

I have never actually seen a toilet seat in real life.

TOILET

↑ Stinging nettles (ouch!)

But I know what they look like because I've seen a picture in the Sellwell Department Store Catalogue – a wonderful, shiny book I found blowing about on the moors one day. I have no idea where it came from ...

perhaps the Person World? Most witches and wizards my age say there is no such place. But I keep the catalogue hidden under my bed and peep at the washing machines and fridges every night. Even if it is only a fairy tale, it can't hurt to dream...

"Hold on!" said Wane. "Hasn't Belladonna already taken the exam for Creepy Castle...?" He gave a nasty little smile. I began to imagine all the things I'd like to turn him into, too.

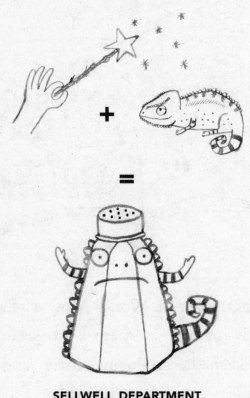

**SELLWELL DEPARTMENT STORE CATALOGUE**
Lizard-shaped salt shaker
*(Page 183)*